# Carved:

## Insanely-Sane Stories

Compiled by-

Pankhi Sarma

BookSquirrel Publication

# Book*Squirrel* Publication

*Regd. Under MSME Act.*

---



All Rights are reserved. No part of this book may be reproduced, stored in a retrieval system, or transmitted in any form by any means, electronic, mechanical, magnetic, optical, manual, photocopying, recording or otherwise, without the prior written consent of its writer.

**"INSANELY- SANE STORIES"**

**By: author name/s**

**ISBN:978-93-89557-64-0**

**Language: English, Hindi**

**1st Edition**

**Formatting: Aditi Gupta**

**Cover: Mr_Ash**

The opinions/contents expressed in the book are sole of the author and do not represent the opinions/standings/thoughts of BookSquirrel

# ACKNOWLEDGEMENT

As the compiler, I'm glad to have this opportunity to lead this project under "Book Squirrels Publication". My first vote of thanks is been acknowledged to the Publication Team for giving such opportunities.

Love to my parents who helped me in completing this on time and of course handled my temper while compiling.

A special thanks to the co-authors, without whom this anthology is clearly incomplete.

And a last vote of thanks to the God for giving this much potential.

# DISCLAIMER

All the stories published under this are original contents from all the co-authors. The characters may be fictitious or based on real events but it doesn't portray any negativity towards religion, language or caste.

As the compiler, it has been ensured that no stories are plagiarised.

But, if found any, only the co-author is the sole responsible.

# CO-AUTHORS

1.  Aarthi Sampath
2.  Abhinav
3.  Anjali Jha
4.  Ankumoni Das
5.  Aryan Verma
6.  Ashtuosh Sharma
7.  Bhojani Ayesha Asif
8.  Deepika
9.  Deepshikha Agarwal
10. Gurbani Gambhir
11. Himanshu Dwivedi
12. Inderjeet Tiwari
13. Ishra Mulla
14. Jarnalisha Sutar
15. Juhi Desai
16. Juman Deka
17. Jessica Bathla
18. Kohinur Ali Khan
19. Komal Kumari
20. Mahalakshmi
21. Manav Gilani
22. Mausum
23. Nikitha S Nair
24. Pinky Ray
25. Prachita Arora
26. Rahul Sharma
27. Richa Chugh
28. Ridhi Nangawath
29. Ruqayya Asif
30. Sai Swaroop J
31. Shobhit Gupta

32.  Surbhi Bhattar
33.  Suchismita Ghoshal
34.  Sumiran Mishra
35.  Sunit Agarwal
36. Tushar Sharma
37. Tushar Ranjan Behera
38. Yashi Paul

## *COMPILER*

Pankhi Sarma, an ECE engineer hailing from Guwahati, Assam is a self – published writer. Currently she has compiled two of her anthologies and has been the co-author of more than 10 anthologies. A blogger, a painter and freelancer content-writer has been into the hobby of writing since her teen days but came in the publishing field from the last year. She has been quite actively involved in many writing communities and also have created her own writing group called writers jugalbandi. She has been also a member of a NGO group formed by her college mates.

A genre of love, happiness, friendship or given any, she gets adapted to all the writing ways. She mainly goes with poetries other than quotes, shayaris or stories.

She can be reached through her Instagram page @pankhi_sarma.

# LOVE COMES WITH SURPRISES TOO

2020 -10th May

Gorgeous walks in!

Nightfall of dancing floors, disco lights, with glorious decor all around.

The red carpet was set up.

Not a gala event. Not a Filmfare. But, it was the college farewell.

Red, black, white, sarees and suits, well shown and neatly tied. All the students came with a proper theme of the farewell night.

Punam, a not so stylish girl but with a properly wrapped back- red saree, big drazzling earrings, tiptoed in high heels to the hall. Alone.

Yeah ...Alone...it doesn't mean she don't have any friends. Rather she came late due to some of her own reasons.

Punam was the CR - Class representative of her class from the last four years. An honored position for her but for all she was not Punam, but a mere CR who only manages events and provided notes on time.

As she steps in, she remembers her first day at college. How she with brave heart entered a cage where she didn't dream destined to.

She survived, she sailed through every sea wave, bigger or lower. She stood drenched during rains and in the scorching heat during summer.

Still, she moved on with the highest and lowest of tides. She never looked back during her four years. She tried to lived the days, to live her destiny with open eyes.

Four years took a toll in her eyes. She saw some of the happening moments and as well as the turmoil of sadness, taunts, insults, failures, all came haunting her for a moment.

Hey Punam, "Looking very beautiful". Someone said. She in her choked voice and watery eyes said thank you and left for the washroom. Smudged eyes wiped off.

A nicely put Kamal and a bit of lipstick and the last touch-ups. She re-entered the hall but a smile on her face and forgotten past.

She soon joins her group of girls. Laughter, selfies, photoshoots went on.

Period.

Punam with her friends was just enjoying the performance by juniors while someone tapped her.

It was Rohan with a sly smile. He called her to get with him at the backseat.

As usual, he started by complimenting her. This time a little more. And his sly smiles seeing her red-faced were just to watch on.

He asked her for a kiss but Punam again smiles off. And he pleads but this time with a condition that some surprise is waiting for her after some time.

Amaze, Punam ignores it on the usual note. They both talked for a few minutes and both parted thereafter.

An hour passed. Seniors were offered soft drinks and snacks. The performance was on. And suddenly the lights went off. With a speech starting with her favourite lines of shayari~

Ae- dil behaal na ho

Tu us noor ko dekh,

Akhir Dillagi ki he toh dard bhi hoga...

Par mohabbat Mei dard na ho aur ,

 Dill de na bethe us ishq ke khatir

Toh phir wo ish hi kya! Janab!!

A familiar voice came in with this Shayari. And an unbelievable scene was there to be seen.

Rohan saying these lines announces Punam's name on come on stage.

An embarrassed Punam unwilling went there guided by a junior, was showered with her favourites rajnigandha flowers.

And there he was, bowing down with his hand towards Punam, proposing to be his better-half thereby.

Claps, whistles, shouts, cheers for the new and happening couple. As finally both were to be together after three years of extremity between them.

Happily, shocked, shyly she blinked her eyes and he kissed her alas!

Teachers, friends, all were spectators of this love. No one complained. Nor said anything to stop that.

All of them had that broad smiling face, expressing their happiness for them.Punam and Rohan. Finally.

And Punam finally won herself.. from them who taunted her feelings, her lameness, her naivety towards people.

A victorious smile was seen over her. Then a CR- not-so-mediocre student alas won the biggest of her dream.

Despite the happiness of getting Job, she was more than happy that farewell night.

Period.

Getting off the stage, Punam kisses her to-be husband Rohan on their sangeet evening.

Year 2027- 10th April.

# Aarthi Sampath

Aarthi Sampath, an Artist based in Chennai India, 38-year-old, has Muscular Dystrophy and uses a wheelchair, she has written lots of articles about herself, and writes to break the stigma. She loves to write about self-love, self-aware and empowering words and have Co-Authored 30 Anthologies. And Compiled 5 including the upcoming Anthologies.

She can be reached through her Instagram page @aarthisampath_

# AN UNFINISHED LOVE

A part of me died, and my dreams were orphaned, "why you want me shiv?" Athira mumbled blinking back tears as she never wanted to let her down, especially in front of the man she silently admired, but Shiv had no words, he just hugged her like there's no tomorrow. Six months back he first met her in a library, her eyes were like Searching love in-between books, and her lips were Speaking the language of silence while her Soul devoured the words Tales of Motherhood the book title read, and then he noticed sindoor on her forehead. when her eyes met him, Shiv smiled, but he saw her moistened eyes and a frown on her face as left the place with the book.

Two months later Shiv met her again at a bookstore, this time She was surrounded by kids who were waiting for her to read them a story, "Athira", a kid called her name and she smiled and waved goodbye ,that's when she noticed Shiv sitting with the kids to hear her story, She's storyteller and visited the bookstore every weekend to read stories for kids, And every weekend Shiv used to sit among the kids to listen to her tales, and inhaling her presence gave him hope, thus he fell in love with her soul,  he admired her whenever she interacted with kids and thought how lucky her kids would be to have a great mother like her. Slowly their acquaintance transitioned to friendship, frequently they used to chat about every book they read ,the reviews and stories another day he asked about her family but she changed the topic to books, so one day after the storytelling session Shiv asked her to have a coffee with him, and she agreed walked along to the cafe a few blocks away from the bookstore, on their way he again asked about her husband, "Why do you want to know me", Shiv?, She asked with pinch of anger in her voice but she couldn't control her tears that kept flowing from her eyes, she wiped her tears, "Can I leave", it's getting late, she told, and when she tried to leave, Shiv pulled her hand in the middle of the road, and asked her story as to why her eyes were moistened every time she was surrounded by kids, "what's with sindoor, are u married?", Shiv asked her, cause he never noticed any ring or Mangal sutra, Athira was speechless tears rolled down her cheeks again, as she spoke, "I wish I could have everything ," Athira mumbled, after a brief silence she told Shiv that she was married but her husband cheated on her that he justified his affair by saying  that she isn't good enough to be called as woman, as she doesn't have a uterus,  Shiv was shocked hearing this and without asking further he let go of her hand. That weekend shiv never came to bookstore she tried calling him but it went unanswered, she was a little upset but kids kept her sane.


 Two weeks later he met her at home. Somehow he got her address from the bookstore, she was surprised to see him but when he proposed to her, she stood still ,he asked her to marry him that he wanted to spend a lifetime with her,  "Why you want me Shiv"?, Athira asked, why you want someone who will never be ready to bear your child,  "why shiv?", Athira asked, and she continued as per log rules of men "a woman is never good enough to be whole without a uterus,? she asked and broke down, he consoled and hugged her, "leave me alone Shiv", she yelled tried to pull away from his embrace but he held her close "Athira, live with me, because I want to be loved," he whispered in her ear, "will you love me", Shiv asked her. I will adopt your dreams, "Athira" Shiv mumbled in her collarbone, live with me Athira, he told her as he wiped her tears. There was a long pause and before she could say anything else, he shushed her and kissed for a brief moment, her gaze never left his eyes that she felt an unfinished love aching to be seen and felt inside out.

# Abhinav Gaurav

This is Abhinav Gaurav. He is pursuing B. Tech from Galgotias College of Engineering and Technology. He is presently living in Greater Noida. He wants to catch up everyone's eyes through his writings. He is famous for his deep words in his writings. He can be reached through Email- rjshayar06@gmail.com

# THE NAKED SOUL

I was waiting on a table. It was a date for me. She could be here anytime soon. It's funny that we had met on Instagram. We were strangers.

Anyway, we started chatting. After about three months, we had now started to understand each other's' feelings more than words could convey. One day, she asks me for a date. It was both exciting and scary for me because I haven't even seen her. I was in a dilemma. Does she like me the way I like her? Are the feelings mutual?

As I ask myself this, a girl comes to my table and asks me if I'm that guy. As I looked at her face to reply, I froze. Her face was burnt. I couldn't believe my eyes. I calm myself anyhow and ask her to sit. We start talking. Before I could ask anything, she starts to tell her tragic tale, that a boy raped her and threw acid on her face, causing it to burn. She said "I don't know what you're thinking about me right now, but there's something about you. You're one of the very few people who understand me. You touch my soul. You see more than eyes could. I don't know what are your expectations for a soulmate but I found a true soulmate in you. That guy burnt my face and raped my body but being with you makes all my scars fade and my soul breathe freely. I want to feel this freeness every day with you. Would you like to be that air for me which make me alive, make me fly, make me feel that still, the world is beautiful it's just a skin which burnt, not my dreams.

After she said this, there was nothing that could hold me back from spending my life with her. Beautiful faces fade away, but it is our bond of understanding, trust and love which keeps us together till death.

# Anjali Jha

Anjali Jha is from a small village of Darbhanga district of Bihar. She was born in 30ᵗʰ September 1997. She is pursuing B.Sc. (Horticulture) from Nalanda College of Horticulture Noor Sarai from Bihar Agricultural University, Bhagalpur. Apart from being a student, she is an avid reader, writer, poet, reviewer and blogger. Her works got published in more than 70 anthologies along with her three eBooks. She is also the compiler of 3 anthologies. She has an exposure of working with different organizations like TSM and Radio Vrishti. Writing helps her to survive in her worst phase of life. Writing is just like breathing to her because when she feels depresses, she uses to write her feelings. She is a dedicated but unpredictable personality, surreal in the way she holds her priorities, and realistic towards her goals.

She believes in herself the most because according to her, it's only you who is going to write your destiny through your deeds and no one can do it for you.

# THE LOST DIARY

Love knows no reason and loves knows no season. Love knows no boundaries and love knows no religion. It's a great feeling between two inner souls which can be felt only by them.

How far will you go to find your love? How far will you go to share the voice of your soul? What you will do if you find some carrier in your love?

Rakhi was from Guwahati and Aditya was from Patna. Both were from different states, castes and with a different attitude. Both were though from two different and distant cities and both met accidentally in Guwahati during a festival of Kamakhya. Rakhi being a permanent resident of Guwahati were free to live there near temple all the time but Aditya went there as a tourist. But we can call it a coincidence or accident that they met there and fell in love suddenly.

Though both were of different attitudes, both were different in lifestyle and thinking but it's only loving that helped them to put together as a whole. Being Assamese Rakhi liked eating fish. She loved to visit high-fi places but Aditya didn't eat fish and all. He was completely vegetarian. He didn't like to roam here and there. He loved to listen to devotional songs. He loved to visit religious places.

But do you know? Love is a thing who never happened with your positivity or similarities of your partner. It's random that can happen at any time.

Rather than being two different mankind's but their soul was made for each other. Their soul was made to be one.

It was a day off Monday. Aditya reached there at the temple before an evening at 5 pm. He walked here and there all alone till night. After that, he was tired and tried to take rest for some time. He started searching for a place to take rest in the night. Finally, he stood near a shop and asked the shopkeeper for the rest house. But he asked him to take rest in his home as there were no places left for rest. He accepted his proposal and went inside his home.

Everyone of his family started giving him service like a guest. In all his family members Rakhi was also one of them. She did all the possible arrangements for him. The whole night he spent there. In the morning he tried to move from there. But everyone denied to give him permission. Everyone asked him to stay there for some days. After that, he stayed there and visited all the places.

In between this Rakhi fell in love with him as when she increased distance with him. Finally, a day before his departure she proposed him. After this, he couldn't deny and he accepted her proposal. Finally, they became good friends as well as a lover.

But now it's time to bid goodbye to all of them.

Finally, after spending 7 days he moved to Patna but this time with different feelings were running in his mind. He was moving alone but he had two hearts which was ready to be one. Before leaving Kamakhya, Rakhi gave him a mobile number and she asked about his number. Now their number exchanged and even after this separation their heart's separation was the same. Even after physical distance, their mental distance was nil.

Time passed but their distance decreased with each passing day.

Finally, a day came when she couldn't resist herself and asked her to come for marriage. He also wanted to marry her. Finally, he moved again to Kamakhya and reached her home. But this time her parents and family were totally socked. They were started thinking about him with different perceptions. Even they started blaming him just saying Bihari and all.

After all these bad happenings with him. Finally, Rakhi came in front of everyone and said to her father that I love him and I want to marry him. After listening to this her father became angry on him and slapped hard on her. She fell on the ground and started weeping. This scene couldn't be seen by Aditya and he moved towards her to lift her. But after seeing him moving towards her, Rakhi's father also kicked him hard and slipped from her room. He also instructed him to move from there without uttering a word and her father shouting on her that how could you think to marry in an inter-caste. We have different cultures. We have different thoughts but how you dare to marry him. After that, he shut the door. Now Rakhi was inside the house and Aditya was outside her home. In this incident, he lost his diary in which he wrote letters and poems for Rakhi. But unfortunately, he forgot that diary completely and rushed towards the temple. He prayed in the temple for her safe stay in her home after that incident and rushed towards the station. He reached to Patna alone with a sad face.

He tried a lot to forgot her but he couldn't. Finally, he moved to Delhi for a job and started working hard and started keeping busy himself to forget her.

Now he moved on track and started a normal life but he couldn't forget her.

Another side Rakhi was keeping engrossed herself in his thoughts. Her conditions were very bad. Her father broke her mobile and sim. She lost all her contacts. She was missing him a lot but she couldn't do anything. She was only remembering him in her blessings. She had one only gift from him was his diary that he lost when her father kicked him. Every day in the morning and in the evening,  she looked at all the writings and pages of that diary. She touched and felt the warmth of his body only in that diary.

Days passed and both were not in contact with each other. Both were living in each other's dreams only.

4 years later it was 6th June when Rakhi decided to set her own life just avoiding her family thoughts and tried to set her own rule in her own life. When she completed her graduation. She started searching for a job to pursue her dreams. She moved here and there for a job interview and finally, she got a job in Patna in a retail chain industry on the clerk post.

Her father instructed to resign her job but she couldn't quit her job and finally moved to Patna. For security, she moved several times to Kamakhya to gain their trust in her.

But another side when she came to Patna. She started searching for him. She tried for several months.

One day when she was travelling from her room to her office. When she reached to office. Suddenly she saw a young guy was moving in front of her office. She ran towards him. She cried his name, Aditya. When she called his name. He turned towards her but he moved forward. Again, she cried and asked from behind about his diary. Then he stood there and waiting for her move.

She reached there instantly and asked him about that diary. He recognized his diary but he couldn't recognize her because she changed completely. After taking the diary he said thanks and moved forward.

Again, she said, "Hey! Listen."

Do you know Rakhi?

After listening to her name, he started weeping and said to her everything. After that, she started laughing loudly. Seeing her like this he asked, what happened? Have you any problem?

She said, "No."

Then she said, actually you remember her so much but maybe you forgot her face.

He said, " What do you mean?

Then she said, the girl whom you are finding is in front of you.

"What?"

"Yes, me".

I am that girl, Rakhi.

"Are you joking?"

No dear I am not joking.

Even after seeing your diary in my hand, you couldn't identify me.

After this, he finally accepted that she is his Rakhi. Both hugged each other tightly and felt the warmth of each other. They spent quality time with each other and asked about his final decision about marriage. He was also ready for marriage. Finally, both reached to Temple and tied a knot of love and blessings of God for seven births. After that Aditya moved to his home along with his Rakhi. Everyone welcomed her arrival in their family and both started living a happy married life.

"Sometimes the situation can change everything in someone's life if they were made for each other then, no one can keep aside them for this sacred bond. They can cross all boundaries whether what will be the situation in their life?"

# Ankumoni Das

Here's Ankumoni Das from a small town Goalpara, Assam. She is presently staying at Guwahati, pursuing her degree in Microbiology. She is an ambivert, who loves to pen down her thoughts and present it to the world. Writing did help her to grow as an individual. She dreams of becoming a Research Scholar and side by side an Author too. Her works can be seen at @scribble_out_ Or can be reached through Email- anko55464@gmail.com

# THE WARRIOR

You don't need Mulan or Pocahontas or Merida to inspire you and give life lessons when you have the most resilient fighter around you; that is your mom. Warrior (n)  The person who is as brave as lion, and who is as tough as iron.  And she is my MOM.  What can be the most heart-wrenching phase for a woman? Miscarriage; Death of her twin babies; Cysts in ovaries; The sentence, "Only one can be saved; either mother or child"; Or Being called a "बांझ".  All these phases are excruciating, right?  It's much more tragic when one woman goes through all these incidents. Can you ever imagine the affliction she went through in those situations?  From my point of view, I think no one can !!  Apart from all these, the most obnoxious period of her life was my birth.  Prior to my birth, if God would forbid, she would be a happy mother of identical twins. But this wasn't destined to be in her life. After that, she had gone through ovarian cysts and one of her ovaries was removed. And the doctors finally declared, "There was about 20% chance for conceiving her next child", which completely depends on luck. God heard her prayers, and once again she was going to become a mother.  But the delivery wasn't that easy cause the baby wasn't in cephalic position. So, during her C – section due to my lower chance of baby's survival, she was operated with a few doses of anaesthesia. Only during the incision, she was given anaesthesia and while stitching she was in her full senses.  This is beyond my imagination what pain did she suffer. If I would be in her place, I might not give birth.  By the grace of God, mum and I was out of danger and thus she proved to be my greatest warrior

# A SHORT-TALE OF A MIDDLE-CLASS GIRL

The middle class doesn't sound good. Well, a girl born in a middle-class conservative family sometimes proves to be a BANE for her life.  She was in her 1st stage of adulthood and had just begun to dream about her future. With thousands of dreams of making her life and her parents' life better, she was admitted to a private college.  It wasn't like that that she was dull in studies, she was medium who one day could support her parents.  But she didn't know what destiny actually planned for her !!  All of a sudden she was engaged and after a few days was her wedding.  Yeah, we heard right," A wedding".  For a girl, marriage is one time. Every girl has different desires, plans for her big day. But for her, it was just a route to continue her studies, to build her career and so that she could look after her parents.   Everything seemed to be a great mess for her. All of a sudden she was put in a whole new phase of her while she never dreamt of.  Thus, walking down the aisle was the only choice left with her for leading a better future.


# UNSPLASHED COLOUR

It was the most waited season "the festival of colours". The whole atmosphere was covered with different shades of colours . The buckets were filled with every couple having the pichkaris in it . The Stage was decorated with marigold and dahlias. The tables at the corner were filled with laddoos, samosa, Dahi vara, jalebi, rabri, juices and all was of her favourite.  As it was her first Holi in her Grandma's House. Everybody was too excited about her arrival.  It was about 11 am, and the neighbours shouted they have arrived from the city. Children were running after their car as they haven't seen such a luxurious vehicle.  Get up, we have arrived at Nani's place, her mother shooked her. She woke up and was desperately waiting to see her Grandparents.  As soon as the car stopped she ran giggling towards them  "nani, nanu, chacha, Chachi" How are you all? Everybody was so happy to see her. Nani said hurry up, and get ready to play Holi.  Saaaraaa raaaraaah. These sorts of noises were buzzing from around and sounds of dhol added much delighted to the surroundings.   She was ready wearing a beautiful white salwar, which was sown especially for the occasion. As soon as she stepped out of her room. Sham called her and said drink the lassi, Nani has sent for you. Without any hesitation, she drunk the drink and set off to play. After a few minutes, she felt mild dizziness and dozed off on the ground. Sham picked up her in his lap and took her to the storeroom. She could feel her clothes were forcefully torn. She felt he dragged her body towards him and the unwanted touches making her body drained of stains.   Thus, from that time onwards darkness engulfed her in its arms and never left her apart. The girl who was dearest to all few moments ago now was treated as ill-repute by the same. She was judged why did she wear such kind of dress that attracts people. Thus, she remained as a living dead for the rest of her life.

# Aryan Verma

Aryan Verma an extrovert, born & raised in Muzaffarpur, Bihar pursuing his Bachelor's degree in the field of Arts. Writing for him is to express his feeling through words. Being a passionate writer, its a dream to turn his passion into a thriving career as a professional writer. Even as a young child he was always conjuring up stories & filling them with colourful characters, sharing them with anyone & everyone who would listen. Since then, he has progressed quite a bit to formulate longer & more complex stories & sharing them with much larger audiences.

You can read his blogs at www.aryanverrma.blogspot.com

# WHAT WILL HAPPEN TOMORROW?

After the day's fatigue, I went to sleep. Just a little while later, I woke up. It was really surprising that a person who didn't get up even after hearing the sound of the alarm got up like this. Well, as per my routine, I got up, went to the washroom, then started brushing and humming my favourite song.

Suddenly I heard my mother screaming - "Look, this boy is still sleeping" "I got up mom!", I said. But she didn't respond. I started washing my face. Again, I heard my mom calling dad- Can you hear me? See what has happened to this boy? Why isn't he responding? He has been sleeping long enough. It was really very strange to hear that I'm here, so why is mom speaking like this? I ran towards my room, then I saw something after which I was shocked for a while. A person like me was sleeping there. "He's not breathing", mom said. "I'm here mom! What happened? Why aren't you talking to me?", I said.

 But, no one responded. There were a lot of thoughts going through my mind. Am I alive? Has anything happened to me? Then after a while, my father said- "Our son is no longer with us!" And then everyone started crying. I was also crying but, there was no one to look at me.  Because my soul was crying, my body had the same paradigm. I was sitting near my body. And I had a lot going on in my mind.

Today is Father's Day, I prepared a handmade card for Dad and thought I would give it by this morning.  Yesterday, when I hadn't my dinner, mom grumbled at me. I also wanted to apologize to her. I used to think every day, I would meet my friends but I couldn't for my own reasons.  It was so bad that a lot was left in my life, because of my "I'll do it tomorrow" type attitude. So far, I left everything on tomorrow and went on moving.

Suddenly, there was a feeling that someone smacked my head gently and said- "Get up son, it's already morning! And how much do you want to sleep? "Oh God! I was dreaming. I mean I'm absolutely fine and nothing has happened to me. I got up fast, hugged my mom and started shouting loudly, I got up!  I'm all right mom! Mom started laughing and said- "Shut up, idiot! I am always with you then how could you not be okay?" But yes, I am angry with you, you didn't had your dinner yesterday. I apologized to her & promised that I would never do this again. I gave Dad the card that I specially made to wish him "Happy Father's Day". I talked to my friends and decided to meet in the evening.

Till now I had left everything in life on tomorrow. But, now is the time to cover and finish all the stuffs today.

Life is too short, if you are missing someone, meet them today. If you have made a mistake, then apologize for it today. If you love someone, confess it today, don't leave it for tomorrow. Because, nobody really knows what will happen tomorrow?

**There are a few moments of life and happiness is to be settled by yourself.**

# Ashutosh Sharma

Ashutosh Sharma, a passionate writer and loves writing mind-bending stories. He has been exploring the beauty of mind since years and now it's your turn to explore this wonderful beauty of mind, be ready. He is a mechanical engineer by profession and done his schooling from Army Public School.

"ALWAYS LIVE UR PASSION".

He can be reached through Email- h99845655@gmail.com

# Mind: A BEAUTIFUL WEAPON

It was one of the usual days of my school, the weather was cool and a bit cloudy. Soon the 3 periods passed and the lunch break bell rang. We all started rushing towards our jumping yard, that 6ft long and 10ft deep pit where we daily used to try to jump over it but we couldn't. But! Today, the results were quite surprising, almost all of us including me jump over it that too in the first attempt itself! I was shocked! I asked to myself and pinched myself, Was it really true! To confirm it, I jumped again and to my senses! I again made it, then I thought why was it not happening earlier; for months we were trying, but why it only happened today that too so easily. The answer to my question was actually in my mind itself, I got it at my home when I started thinking much over it...the only difference I noticed in earlier pit and this time was that now it was covered with mud, and that makes him no scarier or deep which was the only fear before that was stopping us, earlier we were worried/feared that we might fall into it.

So, the question is the pit was the same, the body(me) was the same but the fear was in my mind only and once the mud was there the fear had gone. So, the simple logic is limit/fear was only in my mind! And in fact, that's the beauty of mind, once u fit it with a thought, your body starts to act accordingly no matter what your body's capacity might be up to. In this case, my body was capable earlier also of crossing the pit, but my mind was stopping it due to the failure of falling into it.

So, the mind is a very beautiful thing, whatever u think; your capabilities and body behaviour will adapt to itself accordingly.

Another incident in my life that proves this beauty was that horrible night of 2017 which I can't forget in my life. I was returning from the office, it was raining heavily outside, with lots of lightning. And due to some important work I was too late that night, it was around 10:30pm when I sat in my car, coming back to home but after few minutes my car stopped suddenly without no reason, as it was raining heavily outside so I thought to wait for some time in my car itself hoping that when the rain will become less than will see what was the problem.

But in due time ,suddenly a woman of around my age knocked at my car's window and it seemed she was asking for help, so I opened the window and asked if I could help her and then she asked me to share some time with me and after rain stops she would leave to her home. Being alone I also thought a companion would be better to pass the time rather than sitting idle, so I allowed her to let sit in my car. After some gossiping, I accidentally put my hand on her shoulder but to my shock! it was a terrific incident! My hand strikes on seat as there was complete void and no one was there on the seat, at first I thought I might be in sleepy mood; so after sometime, this time I deliberately fall upon her but this time I was shocked I ended striking a bang with window and there was no one on the seat. I was completely frightened by now ...So now I told the woman to please leave as the rain also stopped and I would like to go my wife and children would be waiting for me ...but to my surprise, the woman told me " hey, James! What happened to you? Are you alright, I am your wife Sienna and what r u telling raining? It's all sunshine outside". And u won't believe to my surprise when I opened the door of my car it was actually sunlight and the lady beside me was my wife only!....so what actually happened was that my wife or another woman? Was it day or night? Was it raining or sunny? Answer to these all questions can only be answered by the beauty of brain.....till then take care and explore the beauty of your mind and do answer me what u think what actually happened that night ! .....

# Bhojani Ayesha Asif

Bhojani Ayesha Asif hailing from Maharashtra loves to read and write novels and poetries. Writing has been her way of expression. She has participated in many anthologies.

She can be reached through Email :
ayeshabhojani5797@gmail.com

# मैं एक लड़की हूँ

वो बाल्कनी मे चाय का कप थामे बैठी थी। बाहर बहुत तेज तूफानी बारिश हो रही थी। पर वो तूफान इस के अन्दर चल रहे तूफान के मुकाबले बहोत कम था। आंखो से लगातर आंसू टपक कर उसकी किताब मे जज्ब हो रहे थे। बारिश की शफ्फाफ बूंदे भी इस के आँसुओं मे मिल कर किताब को रन्ग रहे थे। बल्कनी से नीचे देखने पर उसने देखा के नीचे अफ्रातफ्री मची हुई थी लोग बारिश से बचने के लिये छत की तलाश मे इधर उधर भाग रहे थे। काश ये अन्दर चल रहे तूफान से बचने के लिये छत मिल जाए वो बस सोच कर ही रह गई ।उस के हाथों मे पडा चाय का मग भी पडे पडे ठंडा हो रहा था। पर उसे ये मेहसूस कहां होना था। वो रोना चाहती थी, चीखना चाहती थी। पर वो सिर्फ एक ठंडी आह भर कर रह गई ।कुर्सी पर बैठते हुए उसकी नज़र परोस के छत पर पड़ी। कबूतर को पिंजरे मे क़ैद देख कर उसकी नज़र उसी पर ठहर सी गई। न जाने क्या सोच कर उसने अपना कलम उठाया और कुछ लिखने लगी। वो उस परिंदे से हम्कलाम होते हुए लिख रही थी। या यू कहना बेहतर होगा के अपने अन्दर पनप रहे तूफान को बाहर निकालने की कोशिश कर रही थी ।

क्या अजीब सा इत्तेफ़ाक़ है ये तुम भी क़ैद हो और किसी तरह शायद मैं भी क़ैद हू। हा मैं क़ैद हू, इस सोसाइटी के रीत ओ रिवाज से, लोगों की बनाई गई रिवयतों की जंजीरों से,लोग क्या कहेंगे उस डर से, न जाने कब मैं आजाद हो पौंगी, कोई उम्मीद नही है मुझे बिल्कुल इसी तरह जिस तरह तुम्हे उम्मीद नही है के तुम कब इस पिंजरे से आजाद हो पाओगे। वो कुर्सी की बैक से टेक लगा के आंखें मोन्दते हुए चाय का मग उसने टी पाई पर रखा,यादों की किताब के कई पन्ने इस के दिमाग के पर्दे पर लहराए, वो छोटी थी तब से ही उसे आगे बढ़ने का,पढ़ने लिखने का शौक़ था। एक चाह थी के वो कुछ कर दिखाये। हर क्लास में फ़स्ट आना, कॉम्पीतितिव एग्ज़ाम्स मैं भाग ले कर अच्छे ग्रेद्स लाना। बचपन से वही करते आ रही थी। और आगे भी यही करना चाहती थी।

पर इत्तेफाक़, वो एक लड़की थी। वो लड़की जिस पर समाज ने कई बंदिशे लगा रखी है, वो उन लोगों के दर्मियां रहती थी जिन्हों ने लड़कियों के जात के इर्द गिर्द कई बंदिशे बना रखी थी। वो उड़ना चाहती थी मगर उस के उड़ने से पहले ही उस के पर काट दिये गए ।उसे अपने ख्वाबों को अधूरा छोड़ना पड़ा। जिन हाथों ने जिन्दगी भर क़लम और किताबे पकड़ी थी उन्ही हाथों मे बेलन और बर्तन थमा दिये गए। कहने को वो आजाद थी,पर उस के खयालों को उसे अब पिंजरे मे बन्द करना पड़ा। सिर्फ खुद की परवाह करने वाली वो लापरवाह सी लड़की अपने काम मे मगन रहने वाली,सबसे आखिर मे अपने बारे मे वो सोचने वाली बन गई। किस के लिये???

हां !!

उन्ही लोगों के लिये जिस के वजह से उसने अपने ख्वाब अधूरे छोड दिये। वो कुर्बान होगई,अपने जुनून की कुर्बानी, अपने शोक़ की कुर्बानी, अपने सपनो की कुर्बानी। आज वो एक मुकम्मल औरत बन गई। पर शायद इस मुकम्मल औरत बन्ने के सफर मे उसने खुद की ही ज़ात को खो दिया। न जाने और भी कितनो को इस राह से गुजरना था।झूले मे से रोने की अवाज आने पर उसकी आंख खुली, जहा उसकी अपनी प्यारी बेटी,इसे देखे जरही थी। उसने दिल मे ये सोचा के शायद इसे भी कल इसी दौर से गुजरना होगा। अपने सपनो को अपने ही हाथों से रोन्द्रा होगा। ये सोच कर दो आंसू उसकी आंखो से निकल कर उसकी किताब मे हमेशा की तरह जज़्ब हो गए।

# Deepika G

Deepika G is a person trying to explore the world through love coated words.

She can be reached through her Instagram page @dpka_dpz.

# LOVE HAS TO BE DESERVED NOT EARNED

Sometimes we love to take up foolish decisions ending up with regret.

Here's how I loved and regretted being loved by someone whom I loved the most.

It was not a promised wedding where a group of people will be held together to evidence the couple getting married. It was just us and we did it, "To be there for each other forever and forever no matter what". I was filled with love as you fulfilled me with affection and care. I didn't know how fathers will care for their daughters as I had no experience of being a daughter to my father. Maybe because of that, you got all the priorities in my life. Life was so happy as I had you. I was fooled by you which I don't even realise, even though you have made an open statement on me. I kept coming because I had no other options left. It was not the same situation for you as well, because you have someone to look after you now. You got married to someone else and you got your own family to look at. I kept chasing you like a mad woman just to make you realise that my love was true. I tried to make you understand that you were being fooled by people around. Instead of understanding what I was saying, you called me a fool. You called me a drama player and you said that I was acting to pull yourself to my side which hurt me really bad. One last time I gave it a try to make you realise the truth and I texted you explaining things and you replied  "Stop texting you Bitch", which killed me alive. I was broken completely.

I interfered in your personal not to prove myself but to make you realise that you are in the wrong way. I loved you, I still love you. I fell in love with you, not because you look so good, not because your character was awesome, not because you are intelligent, not because you love me, it's because I loved the way you  love your mom, I loved the way you love your dad, I just loved the way you love your friends. I loved you so much when I could see you care for your family with lots of love towards them. That's when my heart started to beat for you. From that moment to till now, you have been my everything. I couldn't give up on you so easily even though you got married to someone else. Even though you gave up on me.

I still miss you. Though I couldn't figure out the reason. I know am being so stupid. But whatever be it, I still see you as my happiness. I know u don't feel the same how I feel about us. If so u would have not used that word b***h towards me. I remember how we loved and missed each other when we were far away. Now I'm just nearby to you, but you don't even consider me as a person. I'm so mad that I'm like this. I don't know how to make u understand that I was not dramatic or acting. I really loved you. I don't want to explain things which say am right u were wrong either I don't want you to think that you were wrong am right.

Even though you have forgotten and moved on I won't give up on you because I want you to realise that I really loved you. You will get to know about your realisation only when you get certain things without clear explanations corresponding to the situations. That's when you will feel my pain.

I'll pray that you don't even realise and I'll pray that I will keep trying to make you realise and I'll pray that, I should fail in all my attempts.

Certain things are designed in destiny. Certain things don't need explanations. Explained things will get expired easily. For which "Love has to deserved  not earned"

# Deepshikha Agarwal

Deepshikha Agarwal is a tutor who is preparing for bank exams. She has also got the best student of the year and also first rank holder awards in academics. She has completed my masters in accountancy and a writer and photographer by passion. She is a great dreamer who aspires to write about her heart and mind and reach and inspire people. She is a happy go lucky and cheerful girl basically from Haryana, have lived in Assam and currently staying in Bharuch Gujarat since 17 years.

She can be reached via Email-
deepshikhaagarwal111995@gmail.com

# HARD EARNED MONEY V/S CHEATED MONEY

She worked day and night like a machine for them, they were the backbone of her life! One appreciated her hard work and faith over him, while the other just used her and her money! The money she earned was her money, but she used to say that belonged to all three of them! She after knowing the truth of the other one stopped giving him money, while other one gave the information about each and every penny spent by him to his sister (cum mother)! The other one after not getting money from her stopped talking to her, came home late and now started doing wrong things to earn money, while another one who cared topped in his masters in the university and got an amazing job too! A few days later: - the first salary of other one came, he gave the whole amount to his sister! The other one just threw money, in front of her sister like anything! After few years: - both got married, had children; and now it's their time to get repaid! The job one had their children as toppers of their own classes, while the other also got children with great marks but his only single child was kidnapped and killed brutally by those people from whom he borrowed money by bad means and did bad works!

So, karma always plays its role, whether good or bad! Money is money, but hard-earned money gives happiness to all, while the money earned either by the way of cheating or evil works always lead to worst results! So, earn less but earn with your hard work and dignity, so that your family or you or your loved ones do not suffer in future!

# BLEEDING IS AS NATURAL AS BREATHING

She was 15 when she started bleeding. It really sucked her. She used to be an insomniac and very much depressed and nowhere to go, girl. She used to lock herself in a room those 7 days when she was in her periods. She used to take a cut-off from all school, tuition, play, even her karate which she loved a lot. She didn't participate in any events of karate when she used to be in her periods. She really used to love karate. It was her first love. But she ignored it too during her periods. Then one day her favourite teacher came to her house worried while she had not been to school since last 10 days also not participated in any karate championship tournaments. She then came to know about her fear. She with all the hopes and ways stated her how the menstruation cycle works and little by little she gained a little confidence that she can do anything even in periods too. She then made it her aim that whatever happens she would never lose confidence and she started participating in all ways she could. She wasn't afraid of bleeding now. She used to party, she used to participate in all competitions and even go out for trips too. She was too self-sufficient and self-confident that nothing can stop her now.  She is 28 now, after 13 years she is a successful businesswoman, a social worker and an investment banker who not only makes money but also is a great karate champion who has won over 1000's of medals, trophies and now is too very successful in her life.

Thus, she is an inspiration for all girls who are scared to be live openly while bleeding.  Thus, I would conclude this story aspiring girls to be calm and keep care and understand that: -"bleeding is as natural as breathing ".

# A COMPLICATED BUT A CUTE AND COMPLETE LOVE STORY

It was Tuesday, 26th March 2014; scene of an examination hall when she met him for the first time. They both shared the same bench, same initial and same Rashi. She was wandering around to look for her seat and she found a handsome guy dressed in a black shirt, navy blue jeans and reebok black socks, clean shaved which suited him better than a beard. He was sitting in the place where she had to sit. She went and just sat. He said hi!  With a calm smile, the same Rashi u know, the same bench hope u will be comfortable here. She a bit confused about what to say said hi!  With the same calm smile. The papers came, exams started and he asked her whether she knew the answer to an answer he wasn't able to understand. She nodded and showed him her paper, it was for the first time she did this unknowingly. And exams passed and last day he was about to get caught up with the chit, she took it from his hand and twisted and replied to the teacher with no as she wanted to save him, as secretly she had started falling for him. Exams passed and 3 months passed and now it was the first day of her college. She was tensed to be between too many unknown people but guess what she noticed him again same but this time in a red shirt on a black pulsar 7167, the number also memorized just in seconds. He glanced but didn't remember her. Time passed they were in the same class. Time passed and the same scene repeated, then he remembered her. 3 years passed, with too many confusions, heart-breaks and friendships, college fests and too much fun.

One college fest he tried to click photographs but failed and when the photographs came someone said almost all photographs had half him half her. Everything was clear he wanted to get clicked but couldn't. That day she realised he also loved her. She heart started beating faster as she just saw him, the same feeling he also felt and she ran away from there in shyness. He came and talked but again a misunderstanding as she found him close to some other girl and again fighting, numbers blocked no sights in college or tuitions, just ignoring each other.

It was the last exam when she could ever see him. But the exam bell rang and she couldn't see him. She gave her paper and went outside to sit. She saw him she smiled, wanted to express her love but due to all confusions and fights, she thought to be away and walked away without even noticing him.  One of their common friends asked her to go to the playground at the backside of the college. She reached there, he reached there both didn't talk to each other, just ignored again facing opposite sides. And their common friends played their favourite song and all the memories flashed and both started crying and again their hearts beating faster as they came closer and they hugged each other. He kissed on her forehead, then bent on his knees and proposed her, she just without thinking anything said "yes" and that one yes made their lives.

They completed their MBA from the same college, then the same job and then years later they got married and at the marriage day, their friends called them by the names they used to call each other, they both laughed and also tears of happiness came and now she is Mrs Radhika meets Patel and forever and ever his and lived happily together ever after. So, this is how that stupid examination hall love ended to be the most beautiful ever-lasting love story. Today is 26th March 2019 and they are narrating their awesome love-story holding hands in hands-on their first marriage anniversary.

# Gurbani Gambhir

This is Gurbani Gambhir from Pune, Maharashtra(India).

She completed her education from The Bishop's Co-Ed School and is currently studying in FYJC in Nowrosjee Wadia College.

She started writing at the age of 13 as a hobby, venting her emotions out. She feels it's the best way a person can use to express their feelings.

To read more of her works check out her Instagram page - @_words.of.the.heart_

And contact her through email @gurbanigambhir2003@gmail.com

# THE UNBREAKABLE TRIO

Once There were these three friends named Saniya, Varun and Bella. They all became friends after Bella shifted to Saniya and Varun's society in summer. As usual, everything was awkward at first but as time passed by..... Bella became friends with Saniya.  One fine evening, Varun passed by and mocked at Saniya for sitting with "fat" Bella. Surprisingly, both Saniya and Bella laughed. To this day Varun asked Bella if she didn't feel bad and she replied with a no. To this, Saniya added "See! She seems so cool" and this is how their friendship began. After this simple conversation, they started talking more often and hanging out together. Slowly and steadily their friendship grew.  Saniya and Varun were friend's way before Bella came into their lives so they were supposed to be close friends right? But they weren't!! Bella became the reason for their beautiful friendship....... After Bella entered the new society...It changed a lot.

Many friendships were broken and many new ones made. Many fake bonds broke and true ones were formed. Bella thought of herself as is she was one of those fictional fairies in movies....... She felt bad for all the bonds that broke, even though they didn't break because of her but she felt bad and took it upon herself as if it was her fault.  She was in class 10 and was elder to almost all her new friends except a few. Saniya and Bella also had some arguments in the early few weeks of their friendship itself but they realized it wasn't worth it so their problems were sorted out.

 Varun was the youngest amongst these three and the naughtiest person too. He was also a really sweet and good-hearted guy. On the other hand- Saniya was kind of quiet and relaxed, a great dancer and loved reading books. Bella was the moodiest one! A little mischievous and sometimes calm, a little school girl with a different kind of charm. She had that influencing and extrovertish personality but claimed to be an introvert. Ha-ha!

As opposite poles react, these three also did. First Saniya and Bella became besties, then Varun started getting attracted to Saniya. Everything was so weird in their lives. Everyone was in their teenage and lives were tough! None of them understood what to do. Being mature, Bella helped Varun and Saniya in their lives as much as possible.

In between- Saniya and Varun had a few flings which complicated their friendship and left Bella in between to choose because it's difficult to be friends with the person whom you fall for. Those few months were real tests of friendship. Whenever there were joint matches or activities.....The three of them had awkward situations and conversations but in the end, there was the need for a conclusion. So, Bella buckl

ed up, got Saniya and Varun together with the help of a few other friends and helped them understand the importance of friendship and the problem of forced relationships.

 Slowly things started getting normal and better for all three of them. Saniya and Varun became family friends too as their parents worked in the same office. Days passed by and their friendship grew stronger and stronger. Their bond became unbreakable over the years. There were many problems in their way of course! Sometimes new friends, sometimes their relationships but they had managed to understand the value of friendship so all of them had their priorities set! "Bros before hoes right?"  The same way it was "Friendship before Love" for these guys. They grew up together, facing problems but managed to be together even in good times and bad, happy times and sad- None of them gave up on the other two. Even now, after so many years, they still manage to take out time from their busy schedules and meet up as frequently as possible....... People who know them set their bond as an example of friendship. After all, this is what friendship is! The formation of a reliable, permanent and unbreakable bond. If something is really meant to be, it just needs the correct start! These three prioritized their friendship and gave it a head start and now look where they are. They've come such a long way........

 And as Bella said, " I love these idiots because even when the whole world seems to be crashing down, they manage to help me fix it back!" That's what friends are for, right?  This one's dedicated to all the amazing friends and friendships of everyone. Keep in touch, keep loving and be faithful. Hope all the beautiful bonds last.

Much Love,

Bella.

# THE HIDDEN FEELINGS- A PAGE FROM AN A LOVER'S DIARY.

Dear Diary,

I didn't know I was so strong, I didn't know I could be so good.

I absolutely didn't know I had the power,

The power to sacrifice my best friend, the only person who understood me.

My one, true love..It all happened during October 2016. Four months since I started college. There was a guy in our class who was really sweet and friendly. He hadn't dated anyone and neither did he have ideas about the dirty things in the world. He was like that perfect person, a girl with several failed experiences in love could hope for....... but alas! My best friend came into the picture.

My best friend was- cute, good looking, charming, childish, funny, attractive and really gorgeous. I was nothing compared to her.

As everyone said......and deep down even I knew, I was fat, serious, nerd-like and kind of irritating. But this couldn't stop me from controlling my feelings......Ugh!!

So, like the typical stories, go.....ours began the same. I knew my best friend way before that guy entered our lives. So, well obviously we both were closer than he was to us. But eventually, we became friends and then best friends:)

All three of us became really close. Like it is said, bonds of three are Unbreakable, our bond was one of those bonds. We hung out together, had lunch together, went to the same coaching class, spent half of the day together. Even during holidays, we wouldn't leave each other alone, we'd be found at one of our houses doing absolutely nothing. We simply enjoyed each other's company. Even when we'd be on our phones doing nothing, we wished to be together, just because the mere presence of the other two made us feel comfortable and complete. Just in a few months' time, we had managed to create that bond.

Everything was literally perfect until one day..... feelings crept in. The damn hormones were high on life that they exploded and stuck to each other but only of two people, not the third one.........

That guy confessed to me about liking my best friend whereas the same day I had confessed to my best friend about liking him.

And there we were, stuck in an incomplete love triangle.

My best friend was still stuck on her ex and she cared a lot about him and their mutual friends, what they'd think of her if she left him and all. Well, basically she had many reasons for not dating this guy whereas I literally thought he was the perfect guy for any girl, literally any girl would've been blessed to have him.

He was sweet, good looking, caring, kind, smart, pure-hearted.....what not!! He was literally like the perfect guy I could wish for. Above that, he hadn't been in any relationship before so his love would be pure!! I could give him all I had and not regret it all because I'd know that he'd be giving his all too......but uhm!! I wasn't the lucky one here.

We kept our feelings intact for too long but one fine day, when I couldn't keep to in anymore, I randomly confessed to him while talking but to avoid things from getting awkward, I said I wasn't sure and maybe it was just a little attraction. Little did he know....it wasn't!

Days passed by and I knew I didn't have a chance so just for his happiness I started explaining to my best friend, the good things about him and her mind started to change. They spent more time together, got comfortable, felt safe in each other's company, shared hugs and deep talks, etc. I could see them getting closer and closer, day by day, right in front of my eyes. Honestly, it did hurt and I kept my distance but didn't let them feel so. Luckily I knew how to balance and manage things.

I talked to them about each other and understood that my best friend was ready to be with him. So, well........One fine day, when I knew he was ready to propose, I decided to set them up.

On 31st October, a very special day of my life, my Birthday- I set up my best friend and my crush, in my own party!! Yeah, I did that myself.......

Then I didn't know how to feel. I was really happy for them but was hurting deep down, and feeling really bad for myself. And that was also the time I knew we weren't going to be the same anymore.........

That's true because when you look at us now, we aren't that close.....We're still good friends but you know, I like to maintain the distance.

It's true I miss them a lot, but I know that staying away is for my own good.

So yeah....that's all about it. In case they read this one day, I'd like to give them all my love and wish them happiness forever.
The one and only,

Bani.....

31st October 2019.

# HIMANSHU DWIVEDI

Himanshu Dwivedi is a college student pursuing B.Sc(N). A student who is eager to gain knowledge with hobbies of reading novels and write what he feels. Always loves to explore the world and enjoying life. In the love of nature's creation and on the way of learning to create phrases and sentences full of emotions. Also interested less in social and enjoying the world of creativity. He can be reached through Email: himanshubkd@gmail.com and Instagram @the_ventricle_says

# A LOVE STORY

After having such a heartbreak from the person with whom Ansh is in deep love. He tried his best to talk to her again, but she resisted. He tries to ping her up again anyhow, but every effort goes for the lame. A nearly goes in depression after all this but after many efforts by his friends, he moved on and started a different life. He also moved to another city to keep himself away from all those memories. He is a different person now; he stops believing in love. He always tries to keep himself away from girls. He started working more to keep himself distracted. He stops all outgoings. He just confined himself in work & room.

After 1 year while morning walk Divya saw Ansh and really want to talk. (Divya and Ansh are colleagues and work in the same office. Divya had a crush on Ansh but she hadn't yet told him). Ansh rarely talks to anyone on the other side Divya has friendly nature and loves to talk to all and enjoy life at its best. But she had never talked to Ansh may be due to ignorance nature of Ansh. Once due to some office projects in which they have to work as the team made them talk to each other. Also, Ansh tries to avoid all this. But as we all know; we can't change what fate has decided for us. In the midst of the project, Ansh feels that Divya is somewhere different from others. He started talking to her. They became good friends as time passed but till now Ansh doesn't know that one day he'll fall for her. Their late-night texts and calls, their morning walks takes their relation to some different and beautiful phase. They share every good and bad. Divya already found herself falling for Ansh but she knows what he (Ansh) has gone through so she thought it would be better to wait for the right time. Ansh is not yet aware that he too is falling in love, also not ready to admit it that he's.

One day while talking there arises the topic of love... Divya: what's your opinion about love. Ansh: Yeah its good relation but not for me. because I never like people getting apart sometimes without any reason...what about you. Divya: me..love is never wrong, wrong is the person who can't perfectly define that pure relationship. May be first love is that which test our patience, but when we are in love again it's forever. "And this forever is never a lie." She continued, "I know someone hurts you but that doesn't mean that you stop believing in this pure relationship". Take your time..believe me, hurting self due to anyone's deed is just a lame choice you know..!! He replied, yeah all you said is true but I'm tired of holding separation..my heart can't anymore bear this pain. Because everyone whom I love, gets away from me and it just distorts me. Divya: okay! We'll talk about it later. Good night, have sweet dreams and don't be late tomorrow in the garden I had something to tell you. An- okay! I'll be at the time don't worry. Good night sweet dreams. Next day at the garden they both reached at the time, they were sitting next to each other in an open hut bench and to add to the moment it started raining outside which makes it more soothing. Ansh breaking the awkward silence, you had something to say, just say it!

**(Ohh! I forgot to mention it's the day of propose day 7 Feb..)**

Divya without saying anything bent on her knees Ansh- kya hua.. Divya:- shh! (silence in loudest word) JUST listen to me. Ansh- ..! Divya- It's your eyes with whom I'm in deep love. I eagerly want to assess the depth of your eyes. I want to feel the zephyr of your essence...you know I'm just fearless when you are with me..when I talk to you it's the best moment of my day. I just don't wanna hang up ever..I'm in love with everything related to you. Yes, I LOVE YOU..(Ansh can feel the beauty of these words and also all this makes him feel special) But she continued, yes you are the one with whom I want to spend every moment of my life, yes I'm in deep love with you. And believe me, this 'forever is never a lie'. I want to owe you.

I want my name with you. I want to be yours forever. (So, when such a beautiful and pure soul is on her knees and saying all these beautiful words how anyone can resist himself from saying 'Yes') Divya on her knees with a rose in her hands, "Can I be yours?" An- yeah can't resist me from being yours.

I LOVE YOU Too......Ansh makes her stand up with both hands and they hugged each other and there begins a new story…

# Inderjeet Tiwari

Inderjeet Tiwari has completed his Bachelor degree in engineering. He has come from a background where English is still a taboo and he started writing to just improve my English. The thing is now he can see the improvement and confidence in himself

# STORY WITH RED INK

Sneha a 14-year-old girl, daughter of a government school teacher in the village. In a family of three sisters and a brother, she loves to do what society thing is only been for boys. She has been the school's best athlete competing with boys too. She has won awards in studies and other co-curricular activities as well. Sneha has been close to her father from birth. But, being a girl, her grandmother never loved her. She lives in the society which thinks girls are only meant to be a burden. They come in the world to only fulfil the lust of men and handle the family.

Aarush(only brother) always use you tease her because he thinks that he is superior. Even her family thinks that men are superior. She can notice the partiality between three girls and only boy at home too. Her mother also used to take care of Aarush's diet properly. Still, Sneha is well determined towards her interest as she loves to compete with boys in every field. She never misses her school for even a day.

Today her best friend Arti is not present in the class. She is just missing her. Her mind is not in the class. She is just thinking about her and "Why didn't she come to school ?" Somehow, she managed to finish school and decided to go to meet Arti. She called Arti's mom and asked about Arti. She said Arti is not well and that's why didn't go to school. She asked her to see Arti but mom said she is impure now so can't meet anybody. She just can't understand anything. She decided to ask her mom but her mom didn't tell her anything and said it's just a curse for something.

And everything is normal now. But, today she is feeling the pain. She is just sitting with head down. Trying to divert her mind from the pain but this is the pain she has never felt before. She is still thinking about how she got hurt there, and suddenly she heard somebody laughing. She is not in the mood to face anybody. But still, she sees that a group of classmates are laughing on her. She just can't understand anything. Tears roll from her eyes. Her eyes are searching Arti but she hasn't come to school. She sees some red marks on her pants and that intimidate her. Her legs are shaking due to pain, fear and shame. She just can't stand up. She is crying and feeling insulted in the whole class. Somehow this horror day of school end and she managed to come home. The girl who is always vivacious is crying today. Sneha has locked herself in the room and didn't remember when did she sleep. At night her mom knocked at her door and calling for dinner. She doesn't have the courage to face her family too. After collecting all the remaining energy, she opened the door and go to the kitchen where her mom is cooking. She tells her about red marks and thought her mother will show empathy. But Mom shouted at her "Why didn't you tell this me before"? You have impure the whole kitchen. You will face the wrath of impuring the god. Go and have a bath. She bathed and when she comes out to see that bed at the corner in the veranda and mom has strictly ordered her to not enter in the kitchen and some other rooms too. Nobody is asking about her pain. She wants somebody to hug and move hands on her head with love and care. But nobody is coming near her. She just can't understand anything. How that red mark and some blood have impure her. The whole incident has shaken her.

From that day only Sneha's attitude has changed. Now, she has understood that it's wrongly said that " A girl can't be equal to boys." The true thing is "A BOY CAN'T BE LIKE OR COME EQUAL TO A GIRL".

And this red ink is enough to write and show why a girl is superior to the boy.

# Ishra Mulla

Ishra Mulla's words give wings to her own feelings. Her write-ups are for simple people who understand simple words having greater meaning. Ishra is super ambitious and is a travel freak.

She can be reached through Instagram @_wordplay_by_ishra_

# LOVE BEYOND LIMITS

A sudden call changed everything, the call from uncle that granny is not well. Mom went to watch granny but she was no more. I had a slight feeling that there was something wrong but still I consoled myself that nothing can go wrong when God is with us. But then papa told the truth I was shocked my hands trimmed, my voice choked. I had no option left rather than accepting the bitter truth that she is no more. Tears roll down my cheeks than neck and despaired in my clothes. I just wish that I could get up and realize that this was just a bad nightmare. I just wished; I could have done something more for her. I just wish I could live with her more. I just wished my all wishes to come true. But they can't and that didn't. I lost the most precious person in my life, who always found something good in me to appreciate,  motivate and keep me going, who was so kind and generous.

 These kinds of acceptance she had were incredible. She was so talented artist, yet the talents where hidden. The best guide for my mom, so I have to be caring and careful now onwards towards my mom. She kind of shown me what true love is. In the era of sending parents to old age home, her each child wanted to keep her with themselves. She was really an inspiration, in spite of so many ups and downs, she chose to fight for her life and live it to the fullest possible. She was always fun-loving and adventures in spite of so many struggles in her life. I just liked her attitude she had towards life and people. She had even helped people who can't help her back. I just loved her the way she is and  I'll love her memories forever. Everything was alright till yesterday but Today everything is different. People say time can change overnight and today I definitely believed it. Sometimes people ask what is the assurance that all wake-up tomorrow and we think that it's okay not to be assured but believe in God for our future.

But today all the myths have disappeared, my granny was no more this happed in the mid night without much people's notice, without any frequent health issues. She went when everything was all right, she didn't disturb or distracted, she just left with ease. At midnight when everyone is in sleep, she left to sleep and also left us with peace. Realize that some people are important and we will not get them back. We only live once, confess what you feel and live to the fullest. Losing someone who didn't care is okay but losing the one who cared is worst.

# Jarnalisha Sutar

This is Jarnalisha Sutar and she is lives in Jaydev Vihar Bhubaneswar Odisha, India.  As a pre-mature writer, she writes what inspire her the most. She can be reached through Instagram page @whendreamcrystaliizes or via Email-
jarnalishasutar@gmail.com

# THE HALF-MEMORIES

Think about a condition where you love a person whose memories are fading away which indeed you never wanted. This is what happened to a girl at the age of 20, she loved a person whom she met 8 years ago and have lots of memories with. It was always a one-sided love she never confessed him and she never knew whether he liked her or not. Somewhere in the middle of this dilemma, she started making new friends and having a constant brain problem from childhood her memories of him started fading each day she forgets a special detail about him but she didn't give up on him. She searched for him on social media but his name was so common that social media had 72 accounts with the same name, many without profile picture and description. She never knew what to do so when she crossed 19 she stopped searching for him. She knew someday she will forget everything about him and so she decided to write everything she remembers about her love in a book with a lock which is her phone. But one day she met an accident which made forget everything. When she woke up from her coma she could not remember anything but her mother whom she loved the most even more. The nurse around her were shocked to see her laughing the day she woke up suddenly and calling for her mother. She met her and her mother introduced her friends to her which she doesn't remember anymore. She demands her phone and her mother gave her for some time. All she did was checked het WhatsApp and all the other social media app about her friends and family so that she could act like she remembers everything. The last thing which she read was about that boy she loved and the things she has written made her cry as she could remember nothing of that beautiful moment.

It was time 8 years ago from now. She lived in a campus of her father where his father worked too. They were of the same class same tuition but not of the same school. Her school mate was another Punjabi boy named Preet was there common friend and tuition mate. As a child, she never knew about the love she just knows to do friendship with people and her tuition teacher did a job of making her sit in between the two-nought boy Preet and her love. Preet was good in studies just like her but she fell for the guy who scored zero in every exam. The teacher never beat him but she does and every time it was her duty to punish him severely. Beating him was becoming her favourite job which she never knew and soon they become friends. As Rahul said in *kuch kuch hota hain* friendship leads to love as her in their condition. They were the same as Anjali and Rahul from the above movie so I am naming them exactly the same.

So, Rahul has the habit of losing to Anjali and they love fighting for exactly nothing. They won't play without each other they would never be in two different teams; they would never hide at different places and would never leave each other's company. Their friendship made their friends confuse about their chemistry and they started teasing Rahul in the name of Anjali. Rahul wants Anjali to beat him every day as it was his daily routine and never was the day when he missed the chance of teasing her and getting a good beating from her. The only day she got to know that he is teased by his friends in her name is the day of their separation. They forget to exchange numbers and that's how there never breaking contact broke. Some memories still can't be put open as it would become a novel. So here I stop to describe their relationship which can't be open, as Anjali is no one but me and my love of life can't be revealed. But yes, the fact that I have forgotten everything is true and that's what I make open to all

# Jessica Bathla

Jessica Bathla is a happy go lucky girl. Basically, from Haryana and a Doctor in making. She loves travelling and listens to slow songs. She writes as she loves writings but overthinks sometimes. But she writes while overthinking

She can be reached through Email- jessicabathla1999@gmail.com

# MERI PEHLI MOHABBAT

*" Mohobbat"*

When I was a child. I used to make assumptions about love. That love is having goose bumps when you are with that person, being happy with that person and happiness all around. I used to think that my prince /Mr. perfect will come and will propose me on knees.   But it's not a fairy tale.  Life it is.    I had a friend. We met through a common friend. He knew how to flirt, I thought it was love. I felt in love with him  We used to chat for hours. In the starting. He used to like everything in me. But when time passed, he started taunting me as for me love was having a person emotionally with you. But for him, it was not like that.  We met after 6 months.  Butterflies in my stomach  I was a bit nervous and excited too as I was meeting him for the first time after saying yes, the era seemed to be unknown, the streets felt like a pavement of thorns.  Under the fading moonlight of mysterious nights, I walked alone breaking all the ties  Empty hands,  mind full of thoughts.   Crucified heart.  and a cold war within  In between the mess of this heavy turmoil.  My soul cried louder than I ever did.  I let the destiny to take him away.  And then one fine day!  My eyes witnessed a bright shadow,  it was clear and vivid.  Early encounters engrossed me in fear and then I realized the shadow was of my hope.  The shadow was of my relief.  The shadow was the strength with which I,  unwillingly pushed you away.   But somewhere my soul wanted you to stay. You heard my scars screaming your name, And your arrival faded all my pain,  By holding my cold pieces in your cosy hands,  You took me out of this hell  Stitching my wounds  You sucked all my tears out  Your aura made me delighted  That turned my Boisterous life into blissful symphony,  Deep in your arms  I found my paradise Hand were in hands  Eyes were in eyes,  Those stars smiled with a shine.   But he left me in tears  He wanted to pass his time  I was in love  I wanted to stay as a friend as my love was pure. I hurt myself for months then I left him  I made myself strong I moved on from that so-called relationship. I was a stronger version of myself after that day.

Uska to shok tha hard Kisi pe Marr mitne Ka,  uska to shok tha harr Kisi ko hasane Ka

# MERI MAA

" Maa Sab janti hai

Tumhari hasi ke picche Ka vo gamm bhi janti hai

Tumhari  mushkil Ka vo hall bhi janti hai

Tum lakh chupalo usse

Chehra pdh ke vo Jaan jati hai , Maa Sab janti hai"

## Maa

Let's go back to 2015. I was at starting off my " teenage". I was growing. At this age, we all do a lot of mistakes. We think that our parents are the only ones who scold us. So, we maintain distance from them. And that's really wrong! When I was in 12th standard. I came close to my mother again. The one who used to wake up during my exams. Who used to check that I ate something or not? I passed my 12th. She was the one now. Who stood by my side? Who fought with my father sometimes for me? We came closer. I got admission in BAMS so I went there to another city.

She is my emotional queen. We both talk rarely. But still, I know that she is the one who will help me whenever I will be in a bad situation.

"maa Sab janti hai, Tere lie ladna bhi vo janti hai

Tumse tumhari bhalai ke lie ladna Bhi vo janti hai

Maa Sab janti hai"

You all should respect your mothers  They are not less than a goddess.

## LOVE

It's a thing which can't be described in words

"It can be seen between the two lovers

Between a mother and a child, Between clouds and rain

Between best friends , Love is us. Love is you

Love is purest of all"

Through these short stories about love. I will take you to the lives of different people and their form of love.

Firstly, let me take you to the story of Timmy and Jimmy

"Love between two lovers"

Simmy – a cute Punjabi girl. And Jimmy – Punjabi Munda

They had mutual friends. He requested her on Facebook. She did not liked Jimmy. He used to message her. After a few days, she replied! They started talking. After years. They fell in love  She was from a strict family. His family knew about them. Her elder brother came to know about their relationship. And he warned Jimmy to stay away from her. They were so in love that they were not able to leave each other. They went through many tough situations but what made them stay together was there trust on each other.

Vo kehte hai na

"Pyar samay mohobbat zaat nahi dekht ", "Pyaar bas ho jata hai"

After 7 years of their relationship, she is a doctor now. He was a businessman

Still in love. But what's the best thing about them is they respect their family.

They were waiting for the right time to tell her family about them.

"Pyaar ki dor se bandha do Dil", Alag kese ho sakte the

They told her parents. He did not leave any chance impressing her brother.He said yes.They got married.

**After 2 years of their marriage!**

She still blushes to talk to him sometimes. They still go for long drives.True love never gets faded. It gets stronger after each up and downs of life.

Yes " love is purest"

# Juhi Desai

This is Juhi Desai here, who loves to pen down her thoughts, her feelings and her mind, she is basically from Ahmedabad, Gujarat. She is currently pursuing Company secretary(CS).She has taken part in various anthologies and she is currently compiling her own as well. She can be reached through her

Email- juhidesai54@gmail.com

# IN THE DESPAIR WORLD

Trembling was she in the fear suddenly she saw herself in the mirror and started memorizing all the memories that she was having from the world which she never thought she would never in these is going to get settle. After staring herself for a while tears rolled down her eyes, she was continuously sobbing in the life she was living, she didn't find any pair of her own. "Isabella" her mom called out. She quickly rushed out of her room and what she saw was a mere surprise for her she saw the neighbour which was living near the Endrew the person she thought she will never again in her life. She was in shocked asked him, "What happened?", Robert in the bit remorse told said to her that, "Endrew is getting married Bella", Bella in shock, "What?" In that minute she thought that her world stopped, she was a bit shaken, then suddenly she realized that they broke up last month. She replied in the bit choked voice, "It doesn't matter now". Robert asked her, "Are you sure?", She said, "Yes". Robert asked her in a bit low tone, "But Andrew wants to see you for one last time he has requested you to meet him". Bella said again with a bit hard of her voice choked, "But I don't want to, I can't see that face again". Robert said to her, "Yeah I understand after whatever happened it will be a bit difficult for you but please for him and for your love please meet him for the one last time". Bella again by getting emotional and choked said, "OK but for only 15 minutes I will meet him in the Starbucks today at 5pm tell him the same and don't be late I won't be waiting for long". Robert said, "OK I will inform him regarding the meet". Robert left the place for his home.

 After a while she started getting ready for the meet as she stated, she was on time. As she entered the cafe the heart shape balloons were all over the floor, the was a way full of roses, she was on the way walked towards the end of the way the scene she saw was unbelievable, she saw Andrew sitting on his leg with a poster saying, "Will you marry me?", She couldn't understand anything, out of nowhere she asked, "Andrew?", Andrew said, "No one ever can be my better half, If you were not my future, I have always loved you and I am extremely sorry for whatever I have said or done until now, please forgive me, You are my lifeline and you will always be the one, So will you marry me? "by holding a ring in his hand by sitting on his one leg on the floor.


 Bella said with a choked voice by sitting on her knees," Yes". She hugged him tightly, she found out that she has already got her world inside his arms. They both celebrated that is how the tragic love story converted in to the most magical one..

# Juman Deka

This is Juman Deka and is a pharmacist by profession. Recently his worked got published in one of the anthologies as a co-author.

He can be reached through E-Mail- jumandeka47@gmail.com and Instagram @JumanDeka

# THE HAUNTED ROAD

The haunted road is the story resembles between the two arch-rivals Bikram and Arun. Bikram is the CEO of the company Soul craft a software company while his rival Arun is the MD of a company versatile meanwhile after achieving the star performer of the year by Arun, Bikram getting angrier so drinks few glasses and left the function in the midway. After that Bikram get exhausted so his wife Rina suggest Bikram to went to go Nainital for refreshment and their child Dipa and Kunal also forced Bikram to go to Nainital and he agreed finally .after the midway of the road suddenly their cars stop and then they see man repairing his cars then they requested him to help he Tells them that there is garage in between the road so they have to travel by road . After that they reach home and then suddenly they saw the man who repairs the cars reached before them .

After some time it was late night 11 pm and they suddenly hear the crying voice of a baby girl and woman after hearing that Kunal get approach to the sound source and then suddenly he is disappeared and Bikram and his family become frightened after that Bikram wife Rina starts frightening and her breath suddenly stops as she has asthmatic problems even inhalers could not save her then Bikram told the unknown person that that day after the award show he drunks and drive with his partner Rajiv and on the road which they are travelling and on the way Arun also driving with his family when Vikram and  noticed Arun is driving he becomes so angry and he drives the car at the top speed and he tried to overtake Arun so at that moment Arun's car get crushed and hit on the roadside tree after few minutes interval Arun died Rajiv meanwhile runs away from the car and trying to save Arun's wife and daughters but Bikram refused to help and they died and becomes evil spirit and they tried to take revenge by ending Bikram all family and they tried to attack his daughter but Bikram considers and confesses his fault and refused Arun's wife to relive her daughter and somehow Arun's wife and daughter relive her by giving lives and they disappear from that place.

**So, it's my short story for readers if there is found any false then requested to show my false it's a fiction does not resemble with any living personalities.**

# Kohinur Ali Khan

Kohinur Ali Khan is a final year student of Banarhat Hindi Government college. He is obsessed with writing shayari, poem and story. He plays cricket, which is his favorite sports. Most of his friends call him by the name Ramzan Ali Khan.

He can be reached through Email-kohinuralikhan92@gmail.com

# मेरा मुलाकात और एक तरफा प्यार

आज १९-०७-२०१८ वो बहुत अरसे बाद फेसबुक पर आयी, और मैने उनको सलाम दिया। उसने जबाब ना देते हुए कहा -कैसे हो? में बोला ठिक हूँ। जैसे-जैसे उनसे बाते करता गया, वैसे-वैसे मेरे दिल की धडकन बढता गया । उस वक्त मानो में ऐसा महसूस कर रहा था, खुदा मेरे लिए एक अहम वक्त निकल कर केवल हमारे लिए भेजा है, खुशी के वजह से मेरे लब लड़खड़ा रहा था, जब में एसमेस लिख रहा था, तब मेरे मे ऊँगलियाँ भी काप रहे थे, पैगाम जब भी भेजता था, दिल में डर और खुशी दोनो ने दस्तक दिया था, इस तरह चेट करते- करते वो अचानक गायब हो गयी, में सोच मैं पड़ गया, आखिर वो कहाँ गयी होगी, सवाल दिल खुद से कर रहा था? क्यों गयी है कहां गयी होगी, कुछ तो हुआ नहीं , वगेरा - वगेरा! दिल पर अजीब सी खलबली मज गया था, और ऐ सब सोचकर में मायुस होने लगा था, जो चेहरा उनसे बाते करते वक्त खिला गया था, वही चेहरा अब मुरझा सा गया था, दिल पर अजीब सा  दर्द था । बाद चिड़चिडा पन बढने लगा। उसके बाद में उनको एक शायरी लिखा । बहुत अच्छे बद आयी थी वो, बिना बोले ही चली गई, उनसे बहुत सवाल करना बाकी था, मगर मेरे सवालों को उलझा कर चली गाय? जब में ऐ शायरी उनको जैसे ही भेजा ,वैसे ही हरा सिगनल दिखाई दिया। मेरे चेहरे पर ओ खुशी नजर आया प्रति  जो २ से ४ मिनटो के लिए गायब हो चुका था। मैं इस सोच में डूब गया था । कि दो चार मिनट में मेरा यह हाल है तो ओ मेरी ज़िन्दगी में आकर लॉन्ग टाइम के लिए गायब हो जाए तो मेरा क्या हाल होगा।

ऐ सोचते - सोचते उनका एसएमएस आने लगा और बाते होते लगा। तकरीबन हम लोग २ घंटा १५ मिनट ३० सेकेण्ड तक बातें करते रहे। और फिर बातें करते- करते  वह फिर से गायब हो गई। इस पर थोड़ी देर के लिए नहीं बल्कि लॉन्ग टाईम के लिए गायब हो गई। क्योंकि मैंने इंतजार उनका घंटों भर किया । मगर

वो आई नहीं लेकिन यह २ घंटा १५ मिनट ३० सेकंड बहुत ही अहम वक्त साबित हुआ।

# Komal Kumari

Komal Kumari, a student of BA, apart from it, she loves writing & expressing thoughts. Writing & herself is like a couple. She is an introvert, but love nature.

She can be reached through Email : komalmylovekk619@gmail.com

# IMPERFECTLY PERFECT

"Hi! You write awesome. Your poems are the best. In love with your writeups! Would you send me a photo of yours? It's just because I want to see the beautiful face of such an adorable writer! ", rings the notification sound on her cell phone. She unlocks her mobile phone and a message request from an unknown guy named " Aryan"  blinks there. She is somewhat confused after reading the text message. Who doesn't like to hear one's self praise, and similar was the case with her? Out of extreme joy, she sent some of her photos to the unknown boy along with a message, "Here's a photo of mine, please don't misuse it. I trust you and so I have sent it to you, kindly don't shatter my trust. "Aryan's instant reply, "Sure, cuty!"  Days passed, the girl received no text message from Aryan is Sunday morning, all of a sudden, while the girl is scrolling her Instagram account, she notices that Aryan's follow request had been pending since a week. Instantly she accepted the request and begins their countless talks either on messages or calls. The girl began to like Aryan.  It was nearly the same on behalf of Aryan but the intensity of both of the persons were different. Gradually and slowly as the days passed the girl felt in love with Aryan. But Aryan was a bit flirty, he used to flirt with how so many girls he met. Even though some where or the other his heart knew whom it loves.

Aryan and the girl made a daily routine where the girl used to write on the topics sent by Aryan with great love in her heart. This went on and on. One fine day the girl proposed Aryan saying, "Hi, Aryan, I like you from the very first day you texted me. The attraction towards you went on increasing and finally today, I realize that I'm in love with you. "No reply on behalf of Aryan.  Unfortunately, the contact between the two was not long lived. It is completely five years and now Aryan is a grown-up man. "Maa, I already said you that I'm ready to marry the girl of your choice. I know you and papa would have chosen the best girl for me! "says Aryan. " Beta, I want you to meet the girl and her parents the very next day" , says Aryan's mom. "Ok, maa", _replies Aryan.

The two families decide to meet at Vinayaka-a well-known restaurant of Chandigarh.   Aryan is not so excited to meet either the girl or her family. The reason behind it nothing but his love for his "City", he still has the same feelings for her. It's sad that he is unable to know his feelings, he is unable to face his feelings. He's the same silly " Aryan".  As the girl opens the gate to enter the restaurant, silence prevails between the two-Aryan and the girl. Aryan seems to be lost in her eyes and the same is the case with the girl. Both the lovers are in a mute conversation. Aryan's eyes beg pardon of the girl. The girl's eyes put forward countless questions.

Amidst the hush and silence comes a voice, "Ruchi, meet Aryan, your fiancé! " Ruchi is quite confused, she is in a confusion that how should she react? She's in a confusion to smile hard or cry loud.

Before Ruchi is be able to overcome her confusion tears roll down her cheeks. Her tears escape everyone's attention except Aryan's. Offering his handkerchief Aryan tries to lessen his guilt. Ruchi takes the handy and something made her smile at this moment, a genuine smile! The white handkerchief with a print on it makes Ruchi travel down the lane of her memory where she's reading Aryan's text "Ruchi, this write-up of yours is mine favourite. It's the closest to my heart and will always be in future. I promise you that I'll be keeping it closest to me!  "Well ,I'm sure, all the dear readers would like to know what the writeup is, it's :- HE-" What do you want me to be of yours? "She-" Be the sugar in the sweet,  Be the salt in the meat,  Be my love, cause without you I'm incomplete!! "

**~because some love stories are perfect only because it's with thousands of imperfections~**

# Mahalakshmi

Mahalakshmi, from Bangalore, has done her MBA in Finance and Marketing. She was working as an Audit Associate at KPMG, Cochin for a few months then transferred to KPMG, Bangalore. Now, a housewife with a 7-month-old kid. An amateur writer with a passion to learn more. A singer and loves to do craftwork in free time. Passion to learn embroidery but time did not permit still. Hoping to do it soon. Energetic learner of new things. Always having the quest to learn new things and wanted to be a bench mark.

She can be reached through Email-maharsha057@gmail.com

# DEAR MOM

Stepped into a hostel a year back. I did not know how the years passed on. Now it's the time for ENLIGHTENING DIWALI. Since all the mates left hostel, I too had to go home. The home now has become HOUSE without mom.  Two months earlier, she reached God's place due to cancer. It was a uterus cancer. Mainly occur due to meagre quality of the cotton used in napkins that women use.  I had no mood to celebrate. Though, came home. I was seeing her anywhere I roam inside the house. I got a letter handwritten by her.  It stated, Son, I want you to be happy always. I know am on the verge of death.

So, the best to spread awareness of healthy menstruation. Don't feel shy about this. You are helping women to live more. I got tears once seeing this letter.  The next day I heard a voice calling SON WHERE ARE YOU? Yes!!!! It was my mom who called me. She sat beside me and laid down on her lap. She herself took some lamps and lighted and told, you should bring light to women's life like this and went away.  I decided to fulfil her wish. Started research on the material that's used in napkins. After my education, I started a manufacturing company of healthy napkins.  I got up from sleep and all it was a dream.

# Manav Gilani

Manav Gilani is 21 years old and aim to tell his stories to the world.  . This is my first work as a co-author. He believes in being open to people so, he welcomes criticism. Please do come forward and share your views about his work. He can be reached through Email: manavgilani99@gmail.com

# FICTION

"My stories are based on real life." Said Francis wrinkled and shivering, the 68-year old Goan, Francis Barbossa visited a shelter home every week to tell the tales of his characters to physically challenged yet interested kids "They are truly real. They are fiction, but they are true fiction." Continued Francis "But Mr. Barbossa, if your stories are real, how are they fiction?" Bunty, one of the kids sitting on the ground in front of him asked. "I said, the characters are real. Not the story. Story is fiction, a work. The storey imagination. But the characters are from this world, we live. Which is created by someone else." Said, Francis. "Sir, why would you write real characters in a fictional universe of your own figment of the imagination ?" Another kid from the crowd listening to him said.

In the evening, Francis comes from his apartment, in Colva, Goa. He walks a lot. Sometimes so much as he reaches the outskirts. This time wasn't any different. He walked through the outskirts looking at *Kacche Makaan.* He saw an old, skinny man, close Francis' age in Dhoti and Nothing on top wiping his sweat while carrying a larger than life bag. "How can I man like that pick up something like... that?" He wondered to himself. They crossed the path and as they exchanged glances, the skinny admiring Francis and his uber class clothes and Francis, admiring the skinny man's strength. The skinny man walked his way and Francis continued on his path, but Francis couldn't walk any more ahead. He turned around and called the skinny man. "Excuse me? Hello?!" He shouted. The skinny man stopped and turned around. Francis walked to him and looked at him. He saw that the skinny man kept the bag on his head down. He looked a lot like Francis himself. "Who are you?" Asked Francis, not having a clue of the reason why the skinny man looked almost like a lost twin of him. "I am you, Francis." Said the skinny man. "How is this possible?" Asked Francis. "Just like you create characters of real life into situations of your imagination, your stories of fiction. I am you." Said the skinny man in a stoic, yet tired voice. "Wait? What?" exclaimed Francis. "This can't be true. It... it... isn't. I am hallucinating." Said, Francis. His shock was too much for him to bear. He starts shivering. He looks at his hand. He sweats. Francis tries to run away from the man but us helpless. He cannot move. He can't move his foot forward. He can't drag himself away from The Skinny man. "If you are done trying to defy our creator, shall we move?" Said the Skinny Man, mocking Francis stoic manner. "No... No please... I don't want to. I want to go home. Please make me do this." In desperation, Francis looks up and shouts, "Don't Make me do this." In a fraction of a second, they enter a dark, edgy, gothic ground with a lot of marble statues. "What is this place?" asks Francis, still frightened and confused. "Look behind and you will understand." Said the Skinny Man. The Skinny Man moved aside and Francis saw a grave. "Well, it's a good way to keep the dead alive. I find cemeteries, and look for people I find interesting, and make stories on them." This whispered in his mind as he walked ahead and saw the name of the gravestone. It said, FRANCIS BARBOSSA, 1971 – 2009.  It was the day he was narrating how he writes characters to the kids of the orphanage.  His inner turmoil grew. His hands shook as if there was an earthquake in him. He dropped to his knees and looked at the grave and fell on it. He sobbed. "Who is writing the story?" Asked Francis, confused to an extent he can't handle.  "Do your character know that you are writing the story?" Replied the Skinny Man. After hearing this, Francis cried even more. Upon seeing his own death, he shouts to vent off his inner psychological turmoil and confusion. "No…. no… no… no…" He sobbed and sobbed.

# Mausami Ganguli

Mausami Ganguli, a simple girl with some simple yet valuable thoughts. Someone who wants to live her life without any regrets, someone who loves to spend time with her friends and family and can't live without posing in front of the camera while making crazy faces. Reading and Writing are the things that she truly loves, especially when it comes to romantic and horror.

She can be reached through-

Email : anushriyagangulimga@gmail.com and Instagram @Mausami_12

# I CAN'T DARE TO WISH

"Priya, now you look even more cute with that little baby bump!", I told my wife as she was combing her hair. Yes, I still remember that day and each of those words we told each other. My wife, Priya Roy was pregnant and we were heading for a party happily while holding hands. "Aakash, let's just book a cab today, I don't want you to drive!", She told me as I was going to sit in my car but I somehow managed to make her sit in our car. I still cursed myself for doing that. Everything was going smoothly and as per my plan; everything was arranged as I wished. Yes, I have planned a small date for us after that party. "Aakash, now tell me where are we going otherwise.", Priya said to me with those puppy eyes and making pouty lips "Otherwise?? What? Your tricks are not going to work on me okay? Be patient na", I tried to manage her excitement. I could see those sparkling eyes getting more and more excited as we were heading towards our destination. I couldn't resist more and hold her hands tightly and maybe that's the reason I could not notice the truck coming and the truck badly hit our car. The last thing I remember was Priya's screams, the windshield had crashed and all the splattered glass were all over us.

 Soon when I woke up in the hospital, the very first thing I wanted to see was my love and my baby. I somehow managed to reach Priya's bed where she was lying with blood streaking hairs and her face was pale. She tried to open her mouth and only managed to say " I LOVE YOU" I held her hand replying "I LOVE YOU, TOO" while kissing her dull lifeless palms. She took one last breath and leave me alone in this cruel world. I saw those lines on that ventilator go straight and ...

It's been 5 years now and the pain is still the same. Sometimes I wish I would have listened to Priya and booked a cab; Sometimes I wish I would have not planned a date that night but I CAN NEVER DARE TO WISH that I didn't meet her. She was the most beautiful thing ever happened to me.   It's so unfair, how could you never know when you're seeing someone for the last time. It's so unfair to never see your unborn child. It's so unfair to let your loved ones go in front of your own eyes.

But who said LIFE IS FAIR?? NO ONE, RIGHT!?

## Love Do Not See Any Drawbacks!

It was love at first sight when she said, "You don't need to cut your wrist for her. If she leaves you for your failures, she never loved you, after all, love doesn't see any drawbacks." and scolded me very badly for trying to suicide. Even though that was the job of the doctor to scold his patient when they do something wrong but I love Those eyes which were making me feel guilty for thinking to end my life when I have so much more to be felt and they were definitely making me fall in love with her and her words. After some days when I was completely fit and fine because of my wonderful doctor, I finally proposed her, I wished she could see all those arrangements I did for her today in the hospital but doctors told me she lost her eyesight forever in yesterday's accident. But 'I love her!' and I want to let her know this as soon as possible and what could be the best place than this hospital where we started our story?

Oh, and even she said 'yes.'

# MY ONE MISTAKE LEADS ME TO MY LOVE

All it took us was that one "Love you" message which I sent her by mistake. Yes, by mistake, my story started by my one mistake which created a beautiful story of mine. As soon as it hit me that I sent that message to her, I sent another message saying "Sorry, it was not for you!" then got panicked and waited for her to break her friendship with me even though I was dying to tell her those words but I don't want to lose my friendship. I don't have that kind of courage to confess my love because what if she didn't love me back? What if she breaks our friendship? What if she thinks I am one of those psycho lovers? No, No, No. All these thoughts started to pop up in my mind. After 5 minutes my screen flashes up with a message saying "Guess what?! I Love you, too" I read that text for at least 20 times to be sure that it was from her, from my love and yes, it was from her only. There it was my time to do a happy dance when another message comes saying "And who else you dared to send I love you, btw?"

# Nikitha S Nair

Nikitha S Nair writes out emotions raw and vulnerable as and how they are. She can be reached through Email- nikithasnair39708@gmail.com

# MAN, ON THE BICYCLE

Pitter-patter fell the rain on the window of her college library, sitting on the rusty wooden chairs that resemble those chairs in the theatres of Broadway posing as an unseen painting of the 20th century she sighed at the open pages of pathology in front of her. A cup of burning chai, a blessing from the bald man at the local tea shop who often cares for her with a slight taunt about her blooming health. The second-year could not get any worse, she thought as she bore a hole through the vacant pages of her new notebook.

The first year was exciting, if not for the demeaning blows of humour from the passive-aggressive seniors and the impromptu questions from the wise professors at the dissection table which was often a hit of reality as to why she chose the profession. Adrenaline was an everyday visitor as she tried to raft her way through the aggressive waters of anatomy and physiology where grey's and Guyton's became the recipients of her everyday prayers. Even though the cruise was difficult the "land ahoy" moment was one of the joyful cries for her typical Indian family, where she was the only daughter of highly cheerful parents who were not soft with the 'rubbing it in the neighbour's face' comments that followed.

Moving to the second year, life was dull. Professors who cared little about your academic acumen and even less about your curriculum with a blazing passion for knowledge sat upon the chairs of judgement. With very less movement in her brain, she looked outside with the hope of momentary excitement. Two scrawny people caught her eye, under one umbrella in the rain sticking to each other. The chance for a gossip dawned upon her, but who is it? She wondered. As she kept gawking at the slim figurines, she cognized the face of a familiar ally. "Radha?" she wondered. Her sloth of a roommate, caring and wonderful at the same time lazy and sleepy. She remembered the fact that her roommate seldom comes to class, but who was she walking with? That thought bothered her even more.

It was the "legend". He was the popular student from four batches senior class. A wizard in the undergraduate medical class. Quizmaster, best debater, class topper, the adjectives were too many for a fifty-page notebook. Well ' I can be all that too' she thought to herself. As they neared, something about him caught her eye. His demeanour was intriguing and his saunter fast but graceful. His eyes gleaming beneath his spectacles. She couldn't think about the various stages of gliomas anymore. She was hooked to him like a fish on a rod. But what bothered her more was Radha attached to him like a child. Flames of jealousy rose in her eyes; she subdued her neanderthal temptations to whack Radha across her face with her ten-kilogram book. She was always ridiculed for her interests in men who were often mere pawns to satisfy her curiosity. As they came in, his eyes met hers with a warm smile. He muttered something under his breath and walked towards her." Is he moving toward me?? "she panicked. She felt her face burning up as her fears of total irrationality bubbled up. "Can I use the seat next to the charger?" she was baffled by his unusual request to the girl sitting next to her. How can he not see the goddess sitting here? Her inner cockiness muddled. As he sat down, she felt an inner peace settling in her, unlike all the unfortunate endeavours she has had previously with the men of her supposed interest.  She kept her gaze down,  staring at her book as her life depended on it. Letters flew over her head like a radio unable to tune in to a station. She was startled by a soft voice disrupting her inner conflict. " You are the girl from the debate on the blood donation day, aren't you?"  he inquired with a slight chuckle. "Yes, I am" she answered with a vigour that threw him off his usual cool self . "ok" he answered with closely-knit brows . "you were really good " he added shyly. She couldn't register his compliment, she felt as if he was talking in mandarin "Xiexie", she thought to herself. The conversation didn't end there. They talked for hours until it was time for her to head back to the hostel. A conversation that made her believe, human emotions were real and love might just be the most beautiful among them. But the credibility which can only just be debated as humans were volatile beings. As she walked away from him, she glanced at him. Still, on his computer, brows knit together his worry lines prominent, and as she looked on, she saw all of it wash away as he saw the love of his life approaching him. Gaze ahead, she marched on as she hummed the melancholy melody of her unrequited love.

# Pinky Ray

Pinky Ray hails from Hyderabad. She writes what she feels and for more stuff follow her on Instagram @wordsbypinky.

Being a teenager, she has learnt that things which she feels are fictitious for people around her, but who are ready to explore her words are sure that these words can be seen and feel. She can be reached through

Email: pinkyray9546@gmail.com

# LIFE IN A DARK ARENA

Back in those straitjacket days, were a girl was a burden and considered to be an inhuman creature who just is born to burn all the joy! Well in my present life they regret what they use to think about a girl who is born strong and was meant to be the lucky charm. I was born! in the dark furious, rainy evening, but I was so serene and demine. But in there, everyone made themselves, the ghostly creatures of judging a baby girl whom they consider as a curse. except for my mom, dad and a spiritual friend whom you consider to be the ghost! Yes, a ghost! Well, I've been an epileptic they say, but little did they know that I always have a good interaction with my spiritual friend in my dreams. It was great having him around! But when I grew up, I didn't see him often, as I've been entered to the phase where I had to face the uncategorized, soulless creatures, who were meant to destroy my primary respect which was hidden for years...' trust'. I meet people who were in need of faith they pretended, but little did my soul knew that they were in need of my privacy and fame! I always shattered myself and constantly were use to donate me every single me, including my interior privacy to them. But they didn't know the difference between a precious gem and a stone.

 These things were observed by my spiritual friend and one damp night, he appears with the vivid anger which was so scary and he whispers his hot fumes of advice to me saying "girl, you're out of emotions of faith because of your soft-hearted nature every unfaithful soul had to steal your worth for nothing. Go gain them by being an empty, unfaithful like them and gain your strengths by getting them back" he said. But I was giving a lesson of being me, the real me" I whispered'. Then he states a line which kind of is relatable to gain what I've lost without my carelessness, wait! I was careless by giving those damp, faithless souls space, a cosy one, in me! Then these remind me the things they've done to me like, how I was been molested by their grudge and was constantly were raped by their feelings and was caged by them and was caught by my sympathy I've been showing on them'. Tears roll on through my cheeks, these were the tears to tear them apart as they did!  Now, I live a life where every new betrayal feels like a cool breeze of nature, which just passes away so quick. I give a careless carcass to the feelings which I receive from people whom I met before. And all thanks to my angel, spiritual friend, who boosts me up by taking me to his place for a while and the place you call is well known as hell. Me being ambivalent was so beneficial that dark and negative seems to be the brightest ray of happiness and courage. This seems too insane but I'm carved by these things which are happened to me, to make me realize what I deserve the most! After realizing the worth I have, I've been vivacious to seek more by living my life with a hint of furore!

"Sometimes dark side is appreciable when you're all torn by the expectations of being in the brightest rays, which are harmful when overseeing ked to be in"

# Prachita Arora

She is Prachita Arora A  19-year-old small-town girl with big dreams, for her writing has been the best art she is blessed with, it has been her cup of tea since past 2 years, according to her it is the best thing which heals and she too says she writes to heal. After doing anthologies she believes that she may not be doing something big in her life but she is happy and that's why she feels so glad to be a writer.

She can be contacted through Email- Prachitaarora11@gmail.com

# DREAM

Dreams never shattered anyone like this before the way they did to her. Since childhood being an orphan, she always wished to have parents like every other child. Every time a client visited an orphanage, she wished to be adopted but this never happened and after so many rejections when she left all hopes of being a child who has parents, a parent wanted to adopt her and knowing this she was the happiest girl alive and for her, it was her another birth. After all the formalities, they took her with them and after spending 2 hours in the car she finally reached her new home. Their house was on the other side of the road and in excitement she was crossing the road carelessly and suddenly she found a truck coming at her and she got fainted. *All-way silence* After a few minutes she opened her eyes, found herself fine and people gathered at the roadside. Barefoot and sweating, she went down to see what was going on there. She found that her parents lost their lives while saving her from hitting the truck.

# Rahul Sharma

Rahul Sharma from Jhajjar is studying in BA 2nd Year from Nehru College

He wants to become a good writer.

He can be reached through Email: rahulsharma967178@gmail.com

# SEM: KING OF A MAGICAL EMPIRE

यह बात है हजारों करोड़ों वर्ष पहले एक जादुई साम्राज्य की और यह साम्राज्य एक राशवत नामक व्यक्ति ने स्थापित किया था जो कि बाद में इसके दो बेटों के बीच में युद्ध होने से यह 2 समूहों में बट गया था एक था स्वतंत्र गण और दूसरा था तानाशाह गण और दोनों गण एक दूसरे के विपरीत थे जहां स्वतन्त्र गण नियम और अनुशासन में रहकर शासन करते थे और दूसरी तरफ तानाशाह गण सिर्फ हुकूमत चाहते थे दोनों के क्रमशः राजा थे महाराज सत्याहिंसा जादूगर और बुरबुरा जादूगर थे और स्वतन्त्र गण का राजकुमार था सेम जादूगर और यह कहानी इसी राजकुमार की है शादी के बाद यह अपनी पत्नी के साथ एक मेले में घूमने गया था जब यह वापिस आ रहे थे तो इन्हें इनके राज्य पर हमले की सूचना मिली जोकि बुरबुरा जादूगर ने किया था फिर इसको यह चिंता सताने लगी कि ईसका बड़ा भाई यह युद्ध अकेले नहीं लड़ सकता क्योंकि वह इतना काबिल नहीं था और इसकी भी जादुई शिक्षा कुछ समय पहले ही खत्म हुई थी और और इसको राजकीय शक्ति भी प्राप्त नहीं थी फिर इसको इसके सलाहकार ने सलाह दी की यह अपने गुरु राजगुरु को ध्यान करें और अपने राज्य की शक्ति प्राप्त करें और हम बुरबुरा जादूगर के साथ युद्ध लड़ते हैं और यहां राजकुमार सेम अपने गुरु के ध्यान में बैठ जाता है और दूसरी तरफ महाराज सत्याहिंसा बुरबुरा जादूगर का सामना करते है और राजगुरु आकर परिस्थितियो को देखते हुए राजकुमार सेम को राजकीय शक्ति प्रदान करता है और फिर राजकुमार सेम भी युद्ध में हिस्सा लेता है और फिर महाराज सत्य अहिंसा और इसका सेनापति मारा जाता है इसके बाद राजकुमार सेम को महाराज बना दिया जाता है और फिर यह बुरबुरे जादूगर के साथ एक बहुत बड़ा युद्ध लड़ता है लेकिन इस युद्ध में बुरबुरा जादूगर शक्तिशाली साबित होता है और अपने राज्य को बुरे जादूगर के हाथों से बचाने के लिए अपने वरदान का इस्तेमाल करके सब कुछ एक पल में ही कैद कर देता है जोकि राजगुरु के द्वारा दिया गया था जिससे हर एक जिंदा जीव वहीं जम जाएगा जहां वह खड़ा है और राजकुमार सेम की पत्नी को यह वरदान प्राप्त था की जो भी उसे शादी

करेगा वह एक समय के बाद अपना पुनः जन्म ले सकता है और इसी कारण से महाराज सेम अपने वरदान का इस्तेमाल किया और फिर हजारों करोड़ों वर्ष पश्चात यानी कि आज से 25 साल पहले इसने पुनः जन्म लिया इसका जन्म एक कबीले में हुआ जहां से एक बंदरी इसको उठाकर ले जाता है और जंगल में छोड़ आता है वहां से यह किसी तरह शहर में पहुंच जाता है और फिर इसको एक व्यक्ति ले जाता है और इसका पालन पोषण करता है लेकिन यह जब बड़ा होता है तो सब भूल गया था और फिर वर्तमान में यह अपनी पत्नी की आत्मा से मिलता है क्योंकि उसको यह भी वरदान प्राप्त था की मैं अपनी आत्मा को अपने शरीर से निकाल कर कहीं भी भेज सकती है और फिर इसकी पत्नी ईसको सब कुछ याद दिलाती है और बुरा जादूगर भी आजाद हो चुका था और यह अपने साम्राज्य को आजाद करता है और सोचता है सब कुछ ठीक हो गया है लेकिन बुरबुरा जादूगर इस पर दोबारा हमला करता है और इस बार महाराज सेम अपनी पूरी ताकत से युद्ध लड़ता है और विजय हासिल करता है और सबको आजाद करता है और फिर इसको अपने असली माता पिता क पता चलता है और वहीं पर अपने लोगों को ले जाकर करता है अपना राज्य स्थापित करता है।

# Richa Chugh

Richa Chugh, 28-year-old thalassemia warrior, from Faridabad(NCR), Haryana.

Completed her Post Graduation in finance.

A Published author who loves to ink her emotions and writes poems, quotes, microtales on different topics varying from social issues to inspirational musings and also interested in making handicraft items.

A person with crazy mind yet a positive soul is apt to describe her..

She can be reached through her Gmail: rc.inkdiary@gmail.com and Instagram @rc_inkdiary

# AFTERLIFE

Last night in the hostel, studying for the last exam I was anxious and nervous at the same time. It was 11:35 and I had no plans of sleeping. So, I thought of going out for a quick tea and also bringing in some nit bit of snacks to much through the night. Closing my books, I went outside my room. Room no. 309, every student gets a new room every year but I was the lucky one to have 1 same for complete 4 years, that too alone. Lucky right? No one to bug me. My friend circle in college was my laptop, my books and only my room. I was never a friendly person. I won't say I am an anti-social but I liked being alone.

 Moving out of my hostel I crossed the road and made my way towards my favourite tea stall. The place where I spent most of the hours of my day, my college life. Sitting on my usual chair, I looked around. Few students were sitting on a table behind me. They looked like first-year students, I got engrossed in their conversation...

"How's the prep going?, you must have completed the syllabus," the first boy said

"No yaar, I am not able to study, I don't know I feeling very low today" second replied

"What happened, all okay?" The girl sitting with them asked.

"I don't know, I am feeling weird things. I guess something is wrong in my room. I feel someone is in the corridor crying, then I hear pages flipping. But when I go in the corridor to see, I find no one. The strangest part is only I am feeling and hearing this stuff. My roomies are all chill. That's why I called you both for tea"

"Oh! So, our hero is hearing ghosts now" the other boy started making fun of him.

 But the girl turned quiet.  "What happened? Are you taking him seriously"? the first boy was still laughing.

"No Sunil, he might be correct", "Anuj what's your floor and room number."?

"304, third floor, Why?

"That conversation didn't stun me.." I knew what was happening. But I couldn't talk to them...  "Why?? What you mean" Anuj asked scared.

Sunil was quiet now. He could sense Tia was serious so he was scared as well.

 "I heard stories in girls' hostel" "I think what you experienced was the same seniors were talking about" Tia was murmuring

"What, tell me... You are scaring me" Anuj was impatient, so was I.

"Well there was a boy in the first year 4 years back. He was very studious. And.."

"And what??" now even Sunil became impatient.

"Well he was very studious and that's why became a favourite of many teachers. But becoming an eyesore for his batchmates. Students started boycotting him. He was never part of the mass bunk and his visit to the canteen was minimal. Thus, he ended up in his shell so much so his absence was noticed almost after 5 months. At the end of the first year, a buzz was formed that the studious champ was missing and finally his room's lock was broken. It was full of books and just a laptop. Nothing. Absolutely nothing else was there. No one could ever find him. Later it was found that he was an orphan and he got admission because of scholarship that's why no one inquired about him"

"Then" Both Sunil and Anuj simultaneously blurted.

"After the room was opened, several attempts were made but none could clean it"

"What?" Is that even possible Sunil shrugged "

Yes, the room was locked and since then people have seen him and heard him on 3rd floor" Tia sighed

"What was his name? Room No.??" Anuj had many questions.

"Sorry I don't know" Tia was low I stood up. With all my will power moved towards them. And said….

"He was Ronak, Room No. 309" They were shocked.  "How do you know?" Sunil somehow managed to speak trying to find where I was.

"Because I am Ronak"

Was all I could say as I knew it was time.  Time to leave My Past and Move to Afterlife!!!

# Ridhi Nangawath

Ridhi Nangawath  She belongs from Mysore and is pursuing bachelors of business administration. She is a shy introvert; Books are the place she hides and finds herself. Words are her freedom when voices in her head confined her.  Will walk an extra mile for food and for love.  Dreams to change lives through her words doesn't matter it's one's or a hundred's. Spreading hopes more than love!

She can be reached through her Instagram page @The_happytales

# DON'T LET THE MOMENT PASS!!

Today I've realized millions of my mistakes. I never thought I could have been so wrong or unjust.  Following the mad race, even I tried, running behind those momentous joys of life which now aren't with me neither as a badge of achievement or in the memories of others. I am the eldest of the three kids of my parents. I was always loved and given everything.  But my thought process would go as I had been given everything I didn't even ask for. I feel whatever I received, I didn't want it rather I deserved something else, something more.  But today when I look back, I feel so stupid of myself. I was the most privileged child. I had received the best gifts by God. But it's too late to realize now as time has fled but I'll tell you what actually happened.  It was in the morning and I had just slept at four. These city lights never fail to charm the youth. Nevertheless, hearing constant denials from my parents, I went to the party. I wish I had stayed. But, when destiny has planned to knock you off your dreamy world you can't help it. I woke up by hearing my mom shout my name, a common scenario.  She banged my door and I yelled back to sleep a bit more. She kept on banging. Dad had left early for office and my siblings were already in school. I shouted again that she never understands. I cursed her under my breath but stopped when I heard a gunshot.

The air had left my lungs. I panicked, called out for my mom, I didn't hear a word. My heart was in my mouth, I was profusely sweating, my hands were shivering and now my voice couldn't manage to come out of my mouth.  I opened the door out of fear and then I see my mom lying on the floor, there she was in blood. She was shot right beside her chest.  I ran to her, I held her in my arms, grabbed my phone and called the ambulance, assured her she'll be fine.  She on the other hand just told me: " TAKE CARE OF YOUR DAD AND BROTHERS, YOU HAVE TO TAKE MY ROLE, I KNOW YOU'LL DO IT, I LOVE YOU! "  And there she's gone forever.  Like how, why, what, when! My life just changed in the past 10 minutes. From cursing her to seeing her die. Still, when she goes she makes sure to tell me that she loved me. How could I do so much wrong with her? Never ever I understood her agony, pain, emotions. I went on with my own goals, ego, attitude, excuses and my life. I am holding her in my arms. I hug her and cry, so loud. My tears don't stop. I can't breathe, I felt like I am dying too, just then I hear a knock on the door, then again there is a bang. I hear mom shouting and telling me to get up.... and I realize that all of it was a dream.

Happiness has replaced the blood in my veins, I run, open the door, squeeze my mom with my arms.  I kissed and hug her and told her: " I am sorry for everything. I did to hurt you and for all the other wrongs I have done. After this, I won't leave you or upset you. I've always loved you, mom ." She hugs me back, kisses my forehead,  wipes my tears and tells me that I'm still a kid and I need to get going for the day. Mothers are those flowers that expect only love, care and respect.  She is the only one who stands beside you no matter how many times you fail.

So, don't waste your time and go cherish it. Moms love is the only saviour you have, you just need to acknowledge it in order for it to work.

# LOVE IS THERE ALWAYS

Hey Mom Dad, firstly I love you both, so stop panicking seeing my letter. I know I told you to go to a cafe together to read this because I wanted you both to be together while you read it. So, I know it's going to be tough but, yeah, listen to me.  It's been a year since I met you guys. Because of the fact that you parted your ways I was utterly upset. I thought that I wouldn't be welcomed back to that place called home. As it had been broken. I had to go to 2 separate families now. One is Sudhir uncle's flat and other will be Neeti auntie's Farm house. You guys now have new kids. And mom I heard you are a 2 months pregnant lady.

You have your own choices but it's my heart, not a computer that you feed information and it just accepts. I'm sorry I took so much time. Neither had I attended your marriages nor did I pick your calls. I was feeling dejected, alone and unwanted. It wasn't easy at all. Because you had been my world.  Okay, it is still the same. Having siblings was my wish, but now I despise it.

But the day before I met your friend mom, Nikita aunty and that changed the truth of my life.  I said her things I hadn't to. I said I hate you both. I hate the fact that I was born to such people who don't care about me, don't want me, never loved me, nor bothered to think about my wellbeing.  And she laughed out loud. She said that you both were fools to actually give birth to me when the world was against it. I sternly asked her, why would the world be against when you were married! It's obvious that people have kids after marriage, what great did you both do in that!

And she said to me - what proof you have that your parents are married? And then I got irritated. I said aunty what are you even trying to say. She starred right in my eyes and told me that you both never got married.

My world crashed.

She continued and told me that, you got me even before you decided to walk together on the journey of your life. And you didn't want to kill me. You never loved each other but loved me more than anything in the world, bought me all I wanted, gave me all I needed. Never stopped me from following my dreams because you couldn't follow yours. You both craved for love all your life. You pretended for the world but you always were just friends. And after so many years Sudhir uncle and Neeti aunty came in your respective lives and you felt complete. You both didn't want to make me feel bad so you denied the idea of parting ways. It was Nikita aunty who told you both to once live for yourself. And you both for once decided to live for yourself rather than for me. Even then I failed to understand you.  I am so sorry I couldn't see what you did for me. What I meant for you! I am so sorry for punishing you both for sins you never did. I am coming to meet you and your new worlds soon. I am having my exams now. Once I am done with all my stuff here, I'll be there with you.

Thank you, mom dad, for all that you did for me.

Yours, Love

# AND NOW YOU LIVE IN ME

I am shocked, astonished and amazed to be here. Just an inch away from death. And you have left me here alone, wondering and lost. How did you get the heart to leave me?  Oh wait, you don't have a heart at all Six months back, you gave me the most precious moment of my life. I can never forget that breathtakingly look you gave me. Something clicked between us at that very first look. You didn't ask me out for a date  Instead you asked permission with your eyes, All I could say was yes, and we got engaged. Yes, we were that crazy! You always told that our families wouldn't object and you will handle all of it. I  thought you said all of that to make me happy  Until I heard my dad coming into my room and asking me to marry you!  My ears were numb and my mouth froze.  Eyes trickle down with tears of ecstasy.


 When things are too good to be true, you ought to understand that you are surely dreaming! My dream was crumpled when I was told that I have Cardiomyopathy/ heart muscle disease.  A situation where I walk towards my death slowly. I saw you were trying your best to be strong, to be happy, to make me feel alive, to make me feel that everything's going to be alright! I saw you die with helplessness every single moment.  I knew I was not going to make it. You stood by me and were determined to win against destiny. And today, we have won! But still, there is no **WE** in it  You have left me.  Yes, it's unbelievable.

Today when we received the call from the hospital, that we can proceed with the transplant now, All I searched was you, Dad said your phone was switched off and you weren't at home. I thought you would see me off before my surgery, but that never could possibly happen. As now I hear that it is your lung and heart that beats in my body ....... Wait! What on earth did happen? Was my reaction! That morning you were brought in the same hospital after a severe accident and were declared brain dead.

You are such a coward and selfish too. You died to give me life, but you also died because you couldn't live without me.

You knew I will not have the courage to die after hearing about your death because now I carried your heart in me. That was the last thing I had of you!  And now I had to live with it, that is the only way we can be. You are my only love, you are in my body, mind and soul!  I'll always be yours and only yours

# Ruqayya Asif

Ruqayya Asif loves reading from childhood & believes that reading can cure a broken heart. She shares the same love for writing. Public Speaking is her another passion. Being optimistic is her way to life. She can be reached through Instagram @ruqayya_expresses or through E-mail asifruqayya@gmail.com

# THE MYSTERIOUS PIZZA DELIVERY

It was 8 July 2019 when many cities in India were struggling due to water crisis yet Indians were busy to cheer for India in the Cricket World Cup.

A man named, Sunderlal was lying unconscious on his bed. He was surrounded by his laptop, cell phone, diaries, half-eaten Pizza and an empty bottle of Coca-Cola. He hadn't contacted his girlfriend, Riya for the past three days. Earlier they had an argument due to which none of the sides came up to resolve the issue. But on the third day, Riya became concerned, as it was for the first time they hadn't talked for so long. After constantly trying to get in touch with him but to no avail, she ended up in his apartment. What she saw the moment she entered his room was something that no lover could tolerate! Insects were eating him up like he was the most delicious food despite his body smelling foul like rotten eggs!

Sunderlal was a reputed chef in a Five Star Hotel. People were crazy to taste the food made by him. He was the only chef from whom celebrities took autographs. His colleagues were impressed by his down to earth behaviour but some were too jealous of him. Riya couldn't believe her eyes when she saw a printed suicide note peeping below the Pizza Box.

"No one, but I am myself responsible for my death. I was struggling to survive in this selfish world and hence took the  decision to end my life."

The police were informed and the case was registered. Sunderlal's body was sent for post-mortem. The forensic reports claimed that he died due to food poisoning and hence the case was closed!

After performing the last rites of her significant other, Riya locked herself in his room. She wanted to discover the actual reason for his death as she still wasn't convinced that her boyfriend could take such a cowardice step. She started reading his diary which only reminded her of the happier times with Sunderlal. She was weeping like a mad man. While reading, she found a page where he had written about his proposal to Riya.

" Today it's one of the most memorable days of my life. I finally proposed to Riya and she instantly said 'Yes'. I can't express how happy I am. I will never forget this date else she would kill me! I love Riya and my hacking world the most. While hacking is my blood in veins, Riya is the oxygen in it!  I can't live without both. I hope, one day, I will tell her about my 'another girlfriend'."

Riya was in deep thought. She remembered how many times she had tried to ask Sunderlal about his secret work. He always used to say, 'its legal' and the conversation was diverted to another topic. Last time also they had a fight due to his secret. But why he never told her about it? Riya found another diary in his cupboard in which his hacking secrets were written. There was a message on the very first page,

"I don't want to use my skills for bad. I want  to bring the reality of so-called Good People  to the eyes of the world."

Riya had a headache due to constant weeping so she slept for a while.

 ' Help! Please Help!' A boy was screaming loudly. He was locked up in a very messy room. Spider webs welcomed the guests in the room. When the familiar sounds of approaching footsteps became clear, the boy stopped screaming. He was afraid to even make a move. His heart was beating very fast. A tear dropped from Riya's eyes. She woke up feeling breathless. She got up to drink water. She wanted to divert her mind from this nightmare. She found comfort in Sunderlal's journals. She kept on reading it. While reading, she found out that Sunderlal as a child was harassed by his uncle and aunt. He was traumatized by this ordeal and for years he never went alone. Riya finally could conceive the idea of why Sunderlal had 'another girlfriend' and why he was an introvert.

 She quickly glanced at the suicide note. She now had a reason why her heart wasn't ready to accept her admirer's sudden death. She checked the call log of Sunderlal's phone. There was an unknown number to whom he contacted last. It was Pizza delivery boy's number. After contacting that number, she was informed that Pizza was delivered as a gift to Sunderlal from one of their customers. The Pizza boy also informed that the customer was so generous that he pleaded to pack this 'gift' himself. The customer, however, didn't leave his number with them. Riya, however, asked the boy, to inform her whenever this customer visits again.

"Ma'am, he is here. You better come fast; he seems in a hurry."

Riya was waiting for this chance and quickly reached the destination while the boy engaged him in conversation about the cricket. The man had long silky hairs, a mole on the left earlobe. He was dressed fashionably and was holding a cigar in his hand. When he turned around, Riya was stupefied. This was the man, whose picture she had seen on Sunderlal's phone with red crosses. The Inspector, who came along with Riya, entered from behind and arrested him.

In the interrogation process, he finally revealed that he was indeed Sunderlal's uncle and it was he who mixed the poison in the Pizza and kept that printed note so that no one can doubt. He wanted to kill him because, Sunderlal was about to reveal his sex rackets, child pornography and other illegal sites to the media.

" I wanted to keep this as a secret. But how come that bastard come in my way? He suffered because he doubted my ability to guide the secret."

In the Court trial, he has sentenced the imprisonment for life. Riya finally fulfilled the dream of her Romeo. With her quick wit and intelligence, she was able to bring the serious matter of sex rackets to highlights once again. She was being appreciated by everyone.

"We are not here together, but in my heart, you will live forever. I love you. I would have never fought with you only if I knew your reason was so noble." Tears rolled down from her eyes as she was completing her letter to Sunderlal in his diary.

" Love you Sunderlal "

# Sai Swaroop J

Sai Swaroop J. is a professional overthinker, Engineer and Wannabe Musician. His beliefs are - "Give as much, (if not more) to the world as you get" and "When life leaves us blind, love keeps us kind".

# CHILDHOOD FRIENDS

She had contracted Alzheimer's and started progressively losing her memory. Rekha had endured twenty long years of turmoil at her son's place. Every day was a battle, a struggle; be it among the young couple or, the two-raining hellfire upon her for the smallest things. Surely enough, as old age took her strength and memory, they decided to leave her at an old age home.

This was such a relief for her, getting a release from that constant racket. She started to smile more but little did she know what more was coming for her.

One day as she was sitting in the hall, a new inmate was brought in. A familiar face. And sure enough, it was Mohit. She went close to him, wondering if he had forgotten her. But, as soon as he saw her, he jumped up in joy, tears streaming down his cheeks.

Ironically, the place where she was abandoned, became her refuge; with the duo reliving their glory days, reminiscing his boyhood pranks, their adventures, the trips they went together, all about their friends and what they all were up to. They also discussed their lives after they had parted to see how different their lives had been. He had a loving and supportive family, all of whom he had outlived whilst, she had a family that was too busy to take care of her.

He shared his life's joys with her in the process himself forgetting his loneliness. He showed her pictures of his son, who used to be an Air Force pilot.

All the childhood memories and the happiness he shared lit up her soul. Her Alzheimer's was fading slowly. She never revealed it to her son, who occasionally came to visit her.

And, in the end, something very beautiful happened. A few months later, Mohit passed away peacefully in his sleep, and Rekha, a couple of hours after that. All the elderly people in the home were awestruck at this occurrence, as much as grieving for the loss of the two warmest souls among them.

In this chilly, cold world, when even family fades, such unexpected friendships can keep us warm.

# Shobhit Gupta

Shobhit Gupta is a software engineer by profession. He has done Executive MBA, MCA from Delhi University and few short courses from IIT Delhi & IIM Kolkata.  He writes informative articles for magazines and websites frequently. He also writes stories, poems and one-liners as a hobby. He writes, with equal grip, in both English and Hindi. He loves reading, writing, singing, travelling and photography. He can be reached at www.ShobhitGupta.in or a mail can be dropped at mail4shobhit@gmail.com.

# A Different Love Story

Love can happen anytime anywhere to anyone. Mostly it is being considered about girls and boys but does it not happen that someone loves his mother, father, sister or brother!

I had a big fear of dogs since childhood. The main reason was my family members used dogs to scare me so that I pay attention to family values. Another reason for fear was due to one of my cousins, who was bitten by a street dog and he got 14 injections.

When I grew up and started working, my employer decided to send my on-site to South Africa. It was a maiden foreign trip, so the internet was explored a lot. One thing was very common in all research that South Africa is not that safe. But it was decided that I will go and I went.

Upon reaching the country, I get to know that there are a lot of securities measures are being taken care of in every house. One such measure which is common in India is to use the dog as a pet animal.

The house, I was staying in Johannesburg, also had a giant size scary dog. I was first welcomed in that house by him only and my first reaction was to book return flight.

Whenever I used to enter the house or go away, he used to follow me from my room to the gate. As I used to scare of him, there used to be one of my colleagues with me always so I used to feel safe. As time goes on, my fear was getting lesser.

Once my landlord told me that "Our 'Dennis' (yes, that dog is Dennis) wants to play with you. He was alone for the last 3 months because his fellow 'Angel' passed away. Now we are happy to see him happy." But my fear was still there to not allow me to play with him. The weather in South Africa is very unpredictable.

Once I washed my clothes, put them in open to dry and went to the office. After about 1 hour, it started raining. South African rain comes along with the very strong wind blowing. I was scared about my clothes as otherwise; I have to buy new ones soon to put a hole in my pocket. I was very much worried about one shirt of mine, as it was gifted by my dad. He is no more with me so it was his last memoir for me. The way the wind was blowing, my shirt could have travelled to America! In such a condition, going back home was not a good idea.

In the evening, when it was pleasant weather, I went home. Dennis was there as expected. I went straight to collect my clothes but there were no clothes.

I thought maybe some of my neighbours have collected it but when I enquired there was no one aware of my clothes. I could do nothing but was coming back to my room thinking about that shirt.  But surprise! I could see my clothes lying on the floor near my room's door.

I was about to look for that shirt in that heap but I saw Dennis coming with that shirt in his mouth. Oh my God! He saved my clothes.

Frankly speaking, I did not expect anyone including any neighbour or maid. I could not find my clothes so I went to them but I was not thinking that they will do it. And this Dennis did it from me, who was like Dracula from me.

All my hatred, fear everything was coming out from my eyes in the form of tears and what I was having for him was pure love!

I felt so much for the first time and I was not feeling any kind of fear to go near him. I was hugging him. It was the beginning of a new relationship. I got a younger brother.

# A RUSTIC STUDENT

"Hey, you! You will sit in the first row from now onwards." My teacher was ordering me with a frown. To hear her shouting at me was like an everyday affair now.

I came to Delhi, with a lot of hopes and dreams, to learn computers. My hometown was too small to have such facilities. It was the fate of everyone to shift to Delhi or any other major city to pursue any career. I was a very homely guy and never visited other cities alone so I used to have a fear of talking to strangers. In my class, everyone used to speak in English and I was not fluent in conversing in English so my class fellow along with my teachers used to consider me a rustic student. Though I was good at all subjects, my personality was not helping me.

Somehow I was managing in my class but facing a hard time due to teacher and batch mates' behaviour. As our examination time was getting closer so our teacher's punishment was also getting intense. I was not having any computer at home and in class, we have to practice as per our teacher.

At last, the D-Day was scheduled tomorrow after a one and half month of studies. I was very excited about this exam as I heard that it will be done on the computer and the result will be ready instantly.

At the examination, everyone was submitting his or her answer at separate computers. I was done with almost all questions except one. Few have completed their exam and the highest marks till that time were 95, it was a general perception that more marks than this is not possible. In the meantime, I have answered one more question and now only one question was unanswered.

I answered that question and right at that moment; my teacher came near me and whisper me to change the answer to a different option given there. I was not satisfied with her answer and did not change it. She again repeated the same order; I looked at her but could not speak anything and just remain idle. There were other teachers also as it was examination so she could not say anything. She just went away saying "If you get failed, then be ready to confront the consequence..."

There were still 10 minutes left but another teacher came to me and said, "If you have answered all questions, please submit your exam and finish it."

"Please, you do it, Ma'am."

"Why? Are you scared? Or want to change the answers?"

"No, I don't want to change any of the answers"

"Okay then, I am submitting it. Please pray to God for a good score."

I think she said that as a joke but I started praying to God the support.

"Congratulations. You have scored a perfect 100."

I was staring at the computer screen for it may be a dream. I could not decide to dance or scream loud. I was lucky that I stick to my answer and did not change it.

Everyone was looking at me like I have turn out to be an alien.

My teacher congratulated me and I could just say, "It is because of your hard work on me."

She asked me, "So you changed the answer?"

I could see the embarrassment on her face when I said "No, I did not"

# Suchismita Ghoshal

Hailing from a small city Malda, West Bengal, Suchismita Ghoshal dreams high to touch the sky keeping her feet to the ground. She is a philanthropist by heart, a nature lover, die-hard believer of humanity & an avid follower of the supreme soul. Along with these knacks, she is also an avid reader, writer, poet, muser, scribbler, essayist, storyteller & a published author. She recently joined an NGO, "Prayas Welfare Society" to contribute a little to the society.

She can be reached through Email- ghoshalsuchismita019@gmail.com

# LOVE 'ELEUTHEROMANIA'

Some places have their own faces. Whenever we keep our steps there, it reminds us of someone special who has never gone blank from our mind. It's their smile which keeps us cosy in between a bunch of unknown faces. It's their memories that never leave us lonely & it's the moments we spent together which innocently warm our hearts. The most beautiful feelings are hidden in between the true promises & the honest determination of keeping them alive. I too have them!  The last time when it gave butterflies in my stomach was his hands strongly pressed against mine while we were in a cab, felt like in a cage full of freedom. We crossed miles after miles looking at each other for a round of intense gaze. We saw so many things dipped in our hearts. Revealed strange mysteries together.  Travelling is always the best recreation for me but this was something unique. Travelling through each other's hearts & touching the eternal beauty wasn't possible if it wouldn't be a "Love 'Eleutheromania' ". This word was discovered when I was writing a travelogue couple of months ago.


Today I can intensely feel the 'Eleutheromania' in every inch of my life. I feel it for him, & want him to feel it back. He said, "I love you." A pair of shimmery eyes & a ring of warm breathe! A short smile & a long pause! That's it. I was more than fascinated. Some words unheard & unsaid yet prominent through a long silence. Leaving me speechless is always his tactics. I call him magician nowadays for my brain rewinds all his words, promises, gazes, cosiness & of course his sightlessness! One month crossed when the last time he left a soft good-bye kiss on my lips. I found it profound, just like old wine, gets better with age. It was something I can live for, something that can drench my soul in no time & something I was always in search of.  I didn't utter a word when he was in a gap then, a wall of window's thick glass,  standing outside the cab, & bidding me goodbye. I too shook my hands & watched him slowly lagging behind & got vanished in a few seconds. My journey seemed to have a strange vacuum now. I couldn't long for him anymore as he had to go.  Strangely I'm in his city today, but not getting him by my side. He was one of the best 'Trouville's" I've discovered through the journey of my life. I feel both blessed & lucky. All I know he has successfully been able to put his face with my memory of this city. When we travel to a place & forget to have the best thing or eat the best food which is considered to be the significant thing about the place, it always leaves an empty feeling inside us & honestly, he has unknowingly secured that position for me. I surmise the whole situation as homesickness for someone I badly want to be with. It's an irresistible urge to make a journey to someone's heart & create a permanent abode.  I am in a voyage called love; let it be a part of puzzling forest, an endless sea, a mountain full of risky pinnacles, or whatever inevitable, my kind of adventure won't be fulfilled if I don't succeed in hitting the destiny named "him".

'Love' is an unending journey, encircled by the longest journey 'Life', & 'Eleutheromaniac' like me finds celestial happiness travelling in love like a nomad. Our areas are small, not the world; Just like our limited thoughts aren't enough in front of unending possibilities.

# Sumiran Mishra

Sumiran Mishra is a student of class 12th. She's been writing stories since the past 3 years. She's a Kathak dancer and is a crazy music lover. She believes that one should always believe in their dreams and should give their best in pursuing them.  You can contact her on Instagram- @sumiranmishra Or Email: sumiranmishra1234@gmail.com

# I WISH YOU WERE MINE

*Characters:- Tarun Sethi - The male lead. (Mumbai)  Nafisa Khan - The Female lead. (Mumbai) Mayank Sharma, Siddhartha Kapoor, Abhishek Gupta, Karan Chalwa - Tarun's friends.*

• Epilogue –

**[Tarun Sethi]** Sometimes love walks in your life when you least expect and want it to. That's what happened with me. Well, it's not a new thing in this world but it was for me. I had fallen in love with her but I couldn't get her. She became a mere part of my daily life but did I become a part of hers?  The Girl I loved but couldn't get.  Her name, damn that name.

While singing a beautiful-soothing song I was driving on a silent street in Mumbai. Silent street in Mumbai! Strange no? Yeah it is but the time is 4:00 a.m. in the morning that is why it is silent. Then I continued my singing session. When suddenly a white Mercedes came Infront of my car, from nowhere, and it suddenly stopped I tried to pull the breaks but all in vein. Is the person who's driving the car insane? I tried to wear my seatbelt just to save myself from getting injured but it was too late as my car got crashed against that Mercedes. My head jerked and I feel on the steering wheel, my hands left the steering wheel. I tried to open my eyes but everything's around me seems blur. I tried to move but all in vein.  Am I dying? No, not so soon. I can't die so soon. And if I am then, Dear God please tell all my friends and my family that I love them.

***Beep***    ~~I am Dead~~

"I am really sorry, please, please, please once. Please" I heard some girl say. Am I in heaven? And are these angels asking for God's permission to meet me? I am famous here, Wow! Sounds pretty cool.  Then I slowly tried to open my eyes, the first thing I noticed is that I am lying on a white bed. My death bed, maybe. Wrapped in a white sheet, I further tried to look and the second thing which I saw was my Dad. He was sitting beside me, on a chair. His head hung low; eyes closed. What is he doing here? I then looked around, fuck this room looks just like a hospital's room. I am alive. God, Thank you. "I am not dead" is the only sentence which escaped from my slightly parted lips. As I said this I saw my Dad opened his eyes with a jerk. He looked at me with concern. "Tarun beta how are you feeling?" he whispered slowly. I stared at him blankly and it took me a moment to realize what he said. "I.. Umm.. I am fine" I said. He excused himself and went outside, maybe to call the doctor. After five minutes, my friends - Siddhartha, Abhishek and Mayank walked in. They smiled at me, it's weird. Are they actually my friends? Because my friends never smile on me, they just abuse, that's it. "Finally, you woke up asshole" Mayank said. Okay, they are my friends. "We were all so tensed for you" Siddhartha said while sitting on the chair beside me. "I am okay" I said feeling the pain in my head. My head is wrapped with bandages it has fifteen stitches. My other body parts are all safe. "Bhai your head got badly got injured. *Dimag theek hai na?* Why are you sitting so silently" Siddhartha said, chuckling? "I said I am all okay" I gave him a deadly glare. "Karan had asked me to tell him when Tarun wakes up. I should go and call him" Abhishek said and excused himself. Karan is my best friend who lives in Bangalore. As Abhishek left the room, a nurse entered. "Here is your food sir" she smiled showing me the bowl of soup. I hate these hospital foods. Euh. "I'd have to eat it?" I said making a disgusted face. "Obviously you have too" Mayank said. "Okay" I looked away. "Please, let me apologize once. Please sir please" the girl who was speaking earlier again spoke something, outside my room. I thought she was a part of my dream but she was real. "Ugh, she again started her 'Please session'" Siddhartha said, annoyed. "Who is she?" I looked at them. "The one responsible for your accident" Mayank said looking towards the gate. "Okay, and what she wants?" I said. "She wants to meet you" he said. "Oh, but why?" I said. "To apologize, idiot" Siddhartha said. "Okay, call her inside" I casually said. "No, we'll not" he said. "Why Though?" I said. "because we don't want to" he said. "Tarun nobody's asking for your opinion okay, just eat your food and stay shut" Mayank replied almost immediately. I hate him. "You shut up, I want to meet her so call her in, as simple as that" I said. Mayank made a disgusted face and left the room. I heard some voices, maybe he's talking to her. After sometime he came in, followed by a girl, I couldn't saw her face though.

After sometime Mayank entered into my room followed by a girl. I couldn't saw her face because her face is covered with some kind of Nakab (Burkha). As they came in a nurse quickly came inside with them and asked the girl to take off her Nakab. At first she hesitated but then she went outside maybe to take it off in the washroom. She came back in after six to seven minutes.

As she entered my room my life stopped, again. I am dead once again because of her. She was wearing a white colour salwar kameez, her body looked so perfect in that dress. Her lips had a light baby pink colour. Her big brown eyes which had a bit of kajal were staring at me. She smiled weakly. It's creepy but I wanted to stare at her from top to bottom, very slowly - which I did. My friends noticed my reaction that's why Siddhartha coughed loudly. I sat back on my bed properly. She took few steps forward towards me. "Hi, I am Nafisa Khan" she said while extending her left hand for a hand shake.

"Hi, Tarun Sethi here" I replied back, touching her hand for the first time with that hand shake. "So Tarun she's the one who's responsible for your accident and she's the only one who brought you to this hospital" Mayank said, uninterestedly. "I know that" I said. "I am really sorry for that. I was in such a hurry that I just..." her voice trailed off. "It's okay. I can understand" I gave her a small smile. She was about to say something but her phone rang which stopped her from speaking. She received her call, excused herself and left the room. I saw her going away, somewhere deep down I wanted her to stay for a bit but I didn't say anything. My friends teased me for my behaviour but I didn't bother to Reply back or to revert back.

After that day Nafisa used to come and visit me very often. We used to talk a lot about anything and everything. She was really good in nature. We never talked about our personal life instead we talked about movies, books, TV shows, cartoons, our favourite songs, artists etc. It was fun to talk to someone with same interests. I'd started to fall in love with her, I don't know why and how but I eventually did. It was one of the most beautiful feeling in the world. My friends used to tease me from her name and I used to blush like a school girl. Soon I got discharged and came back home from that hospital which put a pause in mine and Nafisa's meetings. I hated it, secretly but couldn't help it. She always stays with me in my imaginary world. She's my nafi in it. I love her so much man.

Me and Nafisa used to talk on WhatsApp it was going good when one fine day I decided to confess my feelings for her. I gathered all my courage and called her. With every ring on her cell phone my heart was skipping beats. She picked up the call after six long rings. "Hello?" I said. "Hey, hi Tarun" Nafi said in her beautiful voice. "Nafisa I want to talk to you in person, I'd want to tell you something" I blurted it out in a go. "Oh my God, same here ya. I too want to tell you something IMPORTANT" she said the word important loudly. "Okay so let's meet today at Five, my place." I said. "Ya, sure. I'll be there" she said cheerfully and we disconnected the call.

Today is your day Mr. Tarun Sethi. Say it and Earn it man.

As the time was passing I was being nervous more and more. "What will I say exactly? How should I start? What will be her reaction? Did she already know about my feelings? Will she say a yes? What if not then what will happen?" all these types of thoughts were coming in my head again and again. The clock strikes five and I was waiting for her. After fifteen minutes my cell phone rang. It was Nafisa's call. I picked it up then and there. "Hey Tarun, I'd have to go for shopping as my mom's waiting for me at the Phoenix mall and I am getting late so could you please come down I am standing outside your building" she said this in a breath. "Okay, okay wait I am coming" I said. I came out of **my apartment locked the gate and I literally found myself running towards the elevator. As I reached the ground floor I** walked to the entrance of the building and I saw Nafi standing outside leaning to her cars gate, busy typing on her phone. "Hey" I said as I reached her. She took steps towards me and "Hi, how are you?" she beamed at me. "I am awesome. How are you?" I smiled ear to ear looking at her innocent face. "I am good, too" she said. "so, what were you telling me? Say it?" she raised her right eyebrow. "No no you first. You were telling me something. You say it" I said. "Are, you say no" she insisted and I nodded in no. "Okay let's speak together" I said and she blinked her eyes in yes. We spoke together "I love you Nafisa" I said and "I am getting married" she said. "Wait. You love what? I didn't get it Tarun" she gave a confused look. But I understood what she said. She said that she's getting married. "Leave mine, you say about yourself" I said and she smiled beautifully. "Yeah. You know what I am getting married to the one who I love the most in the world" she said, her eyes twinkling. "oh" was the only word which escaped from my mouth. "You know what my family was not at all ready for this marriage but YOU" she said which made me confused. "me? What me?" I said. "Are yaar. You remember the day of your accident. I mean obviously you do so yeah that day I fought with my family because they were not ready for my marriage with my boyfriend but after your accident they got scared. They thought that I was trying to attempt suicide when our cars crashed. Which scared the shit out of them and they got agreed for my marriage. So good no? I am so happy that I can't even tell you. Like Finally it's happening" she said happily.

She seems to be very happy. I didn't want to spoil her happiness by telling her about my feelings so I kept my mouth shut. "Oh, I almost forgot it" she said and took out a card from her handbag. It was her wedding card. "here, take this I am getting married next month and you are coming. *Koi "bahana nahi chalega"* she handed me that beautiful card which had two names carved on top of it. It was written "Nafisa Weds Imran" in cursive writing. My eyes were filled with tears but I somehow managed to stop them from flowing in front of her. "I will come" I said, my voice almost on the verge of breaking. "Yeah. Now tell me what you were saying?" she said looking straight into my eyes. I tried to ignore eye contact but when our eyes met at that very moment an unknown tear skipped from my left eye. "Tarun? Are you alright? Why are you crying?" she said shockingly. "No, I am okay. Actually, my left eye is paining, I don't know why" I lied. "Oh *Accha*. Do one thing go and visit a doctor." she said with concern. She believed in my lie, this hurt. When you love someone from all your heart and they don't even catch you when you lie. It's the worst feeling in the world. "Nafi come we are getting late" someone shouted from her car. He must be her boyfriend, I thought. "Okay Tarun I am getting hell late so I'll meet you later. Bye" she said this and then came closer to me gave me a side hug and turned back to leave. I secretly wished that it could be one of those moments when the guy prayed for the girl to turn back to know if she loves him or not but sadly this is not DDLJ and I am not Raj nor she's Simran. In reality I am Tarun and she's Nafisa who's not mine. She went to her car where someone opened the door for her she smiled looking at that person and then she sat inside and left without looking at me even for a second.

I feel betrayed, I feel cheated, I feel so dumb. I love someone who's not mine and will never be. Dear Nafisa, I never wanted us to end but you didn't leave me with an option. You'll get married soon and even if you'll have kids a few years later I'll continue to love you because either I just don't or I do love a lot there's no in-between. She's gone and is never turning back, keeping this in my mind I dumped the wedding card into the dustbin near me, deleted her number. Blocked her everywhere - Facebook, Twitter, Instagram. I have to get her out of my sight, for forever.

And then I came back to my apartment. My eyes are bloodshot red, my head is spinning round and round, my vision is getting blurry.

Nafisa, I Wish You Were Mine.

# Sunit Agarwal

Sunit Agarwal, a 21-year-old businessman from Pakyong Sikkim India.

He can be reached via Email- sunitagarwal42@gmail.com

# THE SECRET OF THE PAST

**Part 1**

After a long time, Samaira used her cell phone, after taping the mobile data icon lots of messages started popping up,

Samaira just replied to the people whom she knew.

A new chat head popped up, after seeing it she found that she had by mistake replied to a guy named Amol though she didn't know her.

Amol was trying to talk to her but Samaira didn't want to talk to anyone. Amol thought that maybe he is being too desperate so he stopped texting her. After someday Amol again texted Samaira. This time Samira replied to her and after a short conversation Samira couldn't stop herself from talking to him and was unable to ignore his messages, maybe there was something in Amol.

After a talk, they became best friends and their friendship became more intense, there wasn't secret between them except Samaira's past. Whenever Amol asked her about her ex-boyfriend Samara either ignored her messages or changed the topic. Amol thought Samaira needs more time to be comfortable with him.

The whole week they used to talk in an amazing way, some about love and some childish one and at the end of every week Amol sensibly asked Samara about her past and Samira used to respond in the same manner.

Even after 1 year, Samaira's past remained a mystery. 53 weeks passed and after Amol asking Samira the same question for the 53rd time Samaira's heart melted and she said that ask me the same question next week I will answer it.

**Part 2**

Amol thought where I waited for 53 weeks, there I shall wait for one another week.

The next Sunday came and this time, Amol called Samaira early in the morning, but Amol didn't receive his call.

Amol thought that Samaira must be sleeping so he dropped a message, On the other hand, Samaira couldn't sleep thinking that how is she gonna narrate everything to Amol.

After bathing at around 11 o'clock Amol again called Samira but this time also she didn't receive his call. Amol saw that Samaira has already read his messages yet she didn't reply. Amol got angry because even after seeing his missed call Samaira didn't even bother to call him back, but he controlled his anger and again texted Samaira- "Samaira, you remember your promise right"?

You have to tell me everything today"

Amol's messages were seen. Now Amol got so angry that even after Samaira is having her cell phone on her hand yet she didn't receive his call.

On the other side, lots of thoughts were running into Samaira's mind. Samira decided that she will meet Amol and tell everything to him because she can't explain him over the text or call.

Samaira texted Amol.

"Amol, today at 9 o'clock I will come at your place and tell you everything wait until then, please u don't come to pick me up"

Amol saw the message and decided to wait. Amol's home was just a 15 min way from Samira's home. Just after the clock struck, 8:45  Amol left for Samaira's place because he didn't find it safe at night, in spite of her denial.

Samira knew that Amol will surely pick her so she departed for Amol's place at 8 o'clock in her Scooty.

Amol was waiting for Samira. The clock struck 10 and yet she didn't come. Amol thought that Samaira was saying something about servicing maybe from there she has left for the house.

 After reaching home Amol asker her sister whether Samira had visited their place or not.

His Sister said *"Nahee Bhaiya Samaira didu nahee aayi"*.

Amol sat on the sofa of his living area and waited for Samira.

Amol called Samaira but there was not any response. Amol kept on texting her. It was midnight then and Amol slept in the living area itself.

The next day when he woke up in the morning he didn't find any response from Samira . With all his anger he left for Samaira's home. When he reached there he found an ambulance and a police van standing outside her home.

Amol understood that something was wrong. He ran into Samaira's bedroom and saw her body hanging on the fan of her room

The mystery remained a mystery

**Part 3**

The moment Amol Saw this he was totally broken, he started crying and then police interrogated him asking who are you?

Amol said police how he and Samira became friends but he didn't say what they had talked about last night. Police told Amol to stay outside as they were investigating there.

They searched Samaira's whole room but didn't get anything.

That night Amol couldn't sleep and he thought of going to Samaira's room and searching the proof himself. From the backdoor, Amol entered in Samaira's room. Even he searched the whole room but he didn't get anything.

Samira one said Amol that she had secret locker behind the dressing table. Amol hurriedly removed the table but he didn't say anything. He stabbed there with his hand for 2-3 times but the wall remained unchanged. Mistakenly Amol's and strike to the lipstick kept in Samira's dressing table. As the lipstick fell, the cover opened and it was at that moment Amol realised it isn't a lipstick but a key, maybe the lockers key. But still, the biggest question was if there is a key where's the keyhole?

Amol then messed up everything in the dressing table but he didn't get anything. He now started staring at the key and he saw 4-digit code below the key.

Amol knew what to do next, keep it up Samaira's mobile and entered that code there.

And then the wall behind the dressing table slide a bit and there it was the keyhole.

Amol saw that there was a diary inside that locker, the diary where Amol can get all the secrets of Samaira's past. He picked up the diary and arranged everything as it was so that the police don't come to know about this and he went back to his home from the backdoor.

It was already 2 in the night but Amol was not in the mood to stop and he started reading the diary.

The diary started like this way;

It was my first day in college everyone wanted to sit in the backbench, only I was the one to sit in front, for a moment I thought nobody will sit with me today. But then entered a cute decent guy and sat beside me. I was surprised to see a boy sitting in front, anyway after a while I broke the silence and ask him "Hello I am Samaira, what's your name?"

He replied as Rohan.


**2nd day**

"Today we both were talking to each other and we didn't notice when the class ended, we exchange numbers today, I was just waiting for his call"

**3rd day**

"Yes, I got a call from him yesterday as soon as completed writing my dairy, we talked a lot, in fact, we had a whole night conversation, it was surprising for me how comfortable I was with him in so less time, oh god! I was made for you now"

So, Amol was reading how their love story was progressing suddenly he stopped at a page:

"Today I and Rohan went for a walk in the park, it was just 8 in the night but the park was lonely. Then 4 guys just approached us circling us from all direction and started touching me, Rohan tried to save me and said Samira you go away you just go away. I wish I didn't run that day leaving him alone."

After then Samaira's diary pages were empty. Maybe Samira thinks herself as a reason for Rohan's death. So, she didn't write further.

Amol now got that why Samira didn't talk about her past. While he was thinking all this, he saw that even if the middle pages are empty there is something on the last page.

The last page was like this;

"Never thought of reaching the last page so early, but life wanted it, amul I know one day you surely read this diary, after that incident I never used to come out of the home at night, but today I call you at 9 and I left for your home at 8, as soon as I came out I saw those 4 guys standing in front of me. They forcefully filmed me, maybe they knew that they are going to be exposed. I could not tolerate all this; I am quitting Amol I am quitting". I'm sorry I couldn't tell you this myself

If possible please forgive me


The End

# Surbhi Bhattar

Surbhi Bhattar loves the writings from the starting but when a hobby turns into passion no idea. Today she loves this job as writing, penning every emotion for everyone. She can be reached through Email I'd:- surbhibhattar78@gmail.com

and Instagram @smiling_girl_forever

# DOUBT OFTEN CREATE SPACE

The year before Shaina shifted to new place Assam from Kerala. Here for her everything new she even doesn't know yet prepared for her upcoming challenge.

After a few months, one day all of sudden her smile fades & way of behaving everything changed though she always respects people, love simplicity and quiet calm nature. Now, her way of behaving changed cruelty, disrespecting, arguing. nature adapted. Why it happened so? And how everything gets back to a normal and she came back to the same zone.

Shaina one day with her friends played a game Truth and dare something. Since everyone completes their challenges very well, only she is left now she got a chance to propose Rahil. Now you all thinking who is rail

Now, you all thinking who is Rahil. She connected with Rahil through her best friend Rohini.

For a few months, Rohini is absent. At that time in Shaina life accept Rahil no one is there with whom she does conversation. Rahil is her second friend with whom she shares everything and what's homework, projects etc., they get both friends to help each other.

Now, one day in the lunchtime Shaina said to Rahil that in her life he became so special after Rohini & her father. And Nowadays I'm having a special feeling for you too "I like you Rahil". Rahil reacted ok and Shaina said please don't do break friendship with me. He said no yaar I'm happy that at least you shared with me, don't worry your friendship remain same.

Might be on that day someone heard their conversation. When Rohini came back after a month doesn't know that 4th person said Rohini all opposite things.

When Rohini came back Rahil & Shaina planned for her surprise party as she recovered so far. When Rahil is busy hosting a party. At that moment Rohini asked Shaina hey listen I want to ask you something. Did she say yes? Is that something between you and Rahil, she said nothing like that but yeah, I said that I like him that's all and he said it's okay. Nothing else between us Rohini.  At that moment Rohini left the party in between Shaina said Rahil asked her what happened to her. As Shaina not getting for what reason she left, after a long time she came.

When Shaina next day went to school, she tried to talk with Rohini just ignoring her. Shaina see the same behaviour every day for the week she waited. Afterwards,

Shaina stops talking with Rahil. Because her way of behaving changes she said to him that sorry give me some space. She doesn't let Rohini to be allowed. So, I need space from you also.

Now after 2 months later when the picnic place Announced from the school side for class 9th and 10th. Then, what exactly happened friend you can't even imagine?? Such a horrible seen it was for both the person Rahil and Shaina. Rohini pushed her friend into the river because from that day many negative thoughts took place in her mind. Rohini actually feeling jealous though Rahil and Shaina came close enough as that 4th person said. So instead of clearing her doubts in her jealousy, she put 2-person life in risk.

Rohini knows that her friend Shaina don't know swimming at all. Although all of sudden Rahil seen that someone is floating, he suddenly jumped into the river to save her life. Since in the hurry he jumped he forget to wear "Safety jacket". Now, what for 1/2-month Shaina admitted into the hospital and when everyone came to know this was all done by Rohini. Everyone starts hating her & even her best friend Rahil also. The person who created misunderstandings between them also left her.

After recovering as Shaina came to knew about her friend Rohini. That everyone starts hating her because of her deeds. She came to knew that this all distracting her and even she can't concentrate on her studies.

Though before the studies leave to come. Shaina went to school everyone gathered asking her how is she now. Accept her friend Rohini although she feeling guilty .what she done?

Then Shaina took a walk towards Rohini and ask her what happened, why she is upset? Shaina said I'm good enough now whatever it's happened in past just leave it. Rohini huge her tightly and putting head into Shaina's arms she starts crying.

She said I'm feeling guilty that what I did with you.

Shaina said forget with me and Rahil whatever it's happened at that time? Will you be my best friend again than only I'm going to forgive you?

I'm also going to convince Rahil too. And none of the 3 of us will ever let our friendship sell.

Then everything gets normal again.

Although they all promise from today, they all clear doubts about whatever it is.

*Moral of the story:- clear your doubts whenever arises,*

*In your mind* ☞

*Be specific with your choices,*

*Often choices turn into regrets.*

# Tushar Sharma

Tushar Sharma is an enthusiastic writer and passionate poet, an engineer by profession. He can be reached through Email- ruhanialfaaz@gmail.com

# A JOURNALIST IN JAIPUR

Like any other shining and busy day, I was working and struggling with the Jaipur's traffic as "The Golden Times " never let you enjoy the day. Yes, I am Shivani Mahajan, the editor in charge at the Jaipur 's the most read and sold out magazine and news channel. In the Jaipur's traffic, while peeking out my car at traffic lights, which resembles with my destiny, sometimes Green and sometimes "The Red", I saw a girl, frightened and innocent hiding her fear with smile rushing into autorickshaw with two men. Though I don't notice people so much it was something attracted me and it seems so relatable. Being stubborn, I have to figure it out.  Following the auto-rickshaw, I reached a very strange place.

"Damn", I whispered and my mind went into plenty of questions.  I saw the girl being lined up among many ones to be boarded into a delivery truck which is looking to take them so far as the truck number symbolize that it belongs to Maharashtra region. I was kind of afraid but determined to reveal - "What's going on here"? As there were no weapons in the hands of four men, my doubt was not clear as water about the scene, which can be related to women trafficking. The call was totally mine. Then I searched my mobile and as I mentioned before, about my destiny, it showed up again, I forget my mobile in my car. And here is me and my situation, which should be handled at any cost. Around 60 women or more lined up with their fear on their face and eyes seeking any help to rescue them. After two-thirds deep breaths, my mind actually worked. I got eye contact with the same girl and sent a signal to detach herself for a moment in another side of the truck.

She somehow managed to do it. Her name was Samaira. She told me that those men are women traffickers, there are 60 alive friends of her and 10 are laid inside the truck already. On asking about the weapons she whispered, there are many, they will not show them until something happens. "This took me to the terror zone. Her Eyes was asking for help but she told me to leave and not to risk my life. Then, I decided not to let those men go freely at any cost. I told her to calm down and circulate the plan to every girl and cooperate with me. I didn't have a choice and I had to take action. Samaira left with same fear on her face, however, she got some hope because of me, and some notes of ₹ 500 in her hand. Yes, I gave it, not to bribe the traffickers but to make them greedy for more.  The witty but risky trick, I learned it while covering up many stories about movies. Hell, it was a real story this time and it was happening with me. She fell some notes on the ground and tell those men that she founded them on another side, from a bag full of notes. Then, as expected two of them were greedy and rushed to grab all of the notes, leaving two of them left behind who were not paying so much attention to women . Fortunately, I got into the driver seat outwitting the two of them who were busy in commanding the women.

Also, I found the weapons by the side of the driver seat but I didn't know to use them. I am a journalist, not a cop. Then one of the women pretends to be having a heart attack, shouting and fell down. The two men left behind ran to her and in the meantime, I signalled them to get into the truck. They surrounded the man and quickly got into the truck kicking those men out. I started the truck and drive wherever I found the way and left those men running behind. That was the most dangerous ride that was happened to me ever. And Yes, I am happy as there was no traffic light on this way but the men were still following me. I ended up parking the truck next to the Police station,  and I informed the inspector in charge ."Whoa" what a relief. The smile came eventually onto my face but this is not the last. Suddenly the inspector came to me with lady officers and instructed me in a commanding tone " You're under arrest"? I was never so shocked in my life. On asking he stated that "Those men informed that you are a drug dealer as well as women trafficker. We found weapons, drug and women in the truck which you were driving. Neither you have your ID card nor your any contact. So, you are under arrest."  My words were literally like -" Holy shit! They have drugs also Yes;  I don't have a Dimity left it in my car but that doesn't mean I am the culprit". " See you in court " He commanded.

The whole career was in danger and seems to worthless. Then I realize while crossing a mirror that every time I go on ang report, I switch on my shirt micro camera ."Dam", I sighed. I stopped them and requested the policeman to visit my car left on the other side. We moved to the car and I showed them the ID, phone connected to the camera and its recordings. They understand the situation and released me. "Sorry and thank you for your help in capturing these criminals." - The inspector said with warm nature and arrested the men.

"WHOOA", it was never forgetting the experience. The smile and a thanksgiving gesture showed how those women were feeling.! "Uff", the bravest thing I have ever done in my reel and real life. Yet, there was a camera, I didn't want to show it to the world. It was something personal to save those women . I moved to the office and got a very bad criticism about being late however, I was happy inside.

A day of this journalist in Jaipur was never so awesome.  ~~~

# Tushar Ranjan Behera

Tushar Ranjan Behera Is an Aspiring Writer from Jatni, Odisha. He Is Currently Pursuing His Bachelors in Bioinformatics. He Wishes to Be an IAS Officer. A Writer by Chance. He Is Very Fond of Arijit Singh's Magical Voice. He Is A Part Of 8 Anthologies till Now. Founder of Comforting Words. Instagram - @tush._.writes

He can be reached through Email : tusharran43@gmail.com

# मेरे प्यार को एक पत्र

हेय लव,

आज बड़े दिनों बाद तेरी याद आई, पता है थोड़ा सा अटपटा लगता है। पर सच तो यही है के तेरी याद मुझे रोज़ नहीं आती। पर हाँ याद आती ज़रूर है। पुछेगी नहीं ये सब हुआ कैसे। चलो बता ही देता हुण। अब तुझसे क्या छिपाना। वैसे तो रोज़ ही ट्रेन में सफर करता ह, पर आज एक अरसे के बाद हमारी वाली उस स्पेशल ट्रेन से सफर करने का मौका मिला। वैसे मुझे लगता तो नहीं कि तू कुछ भूली है। पर फिर भी याद दिलाना फ़र्ज़ बनता है मेरा। ये वही ट्रेन है जिसमें बैठ हमारी कई लड़ाइयां भी हुई है और कई हसीन मौके भी नसीब हुए है। ये वही ट्रेन है जिसमें सफ़र करते वक़्त तुझसे रोज़ बाते होती थि, और तू हमेशा रूठ जाया करती थी। कम्बख्त शोर ही उतनी होती थी के सहा भी न जाए। चलो फ्लैशबैक से हकीकत पर आते है। सफर के दौरान जब भी मेरी नज़रें बाहर खुले मैदानों पर पड़ती थी तब तेरी याद आती थी। क्यों उस वक़्त तुझसे बात करने के चक्कर में इन नज़ारों को बड़ा इग्नोर किया था हुमणे। वैसे हम दोनों के बीच अब बाते ही कहा होती है जो इन नज़ारों को इग्नोर कर पाट। बस आँखों के सामने फिल्म चल रही थी हम दोनों की। हम भी ना कितने नादान थे, जो यह सोच बैठे थे के हमेशा साथ रहेंगे। कोई बात नहीं ज़िन्दगी का तो ऊसूल ही है हमारे सपनो को तोड़ना। वैसे मैं यह खत लिख तो रहा हु पर मैं भी इस हकीकत से अंजान नहीं के ये खत कभी तुझ तक पहुचेगा ही नहीं। बस दुआ यही है के तू खुश रहे और हमेशा न सही पर हमे याद करती रहे। मेरी तरफ से ढेर सारा प्यार।।

# Yashi Paul

Yashi Paul, a 14 years passionate, enthusiastic and energetic learner and player. I keep myself busy in writing poems, short stories or quote is also involved in swimming, basketball, drawing and dance including study. In future she wants to be a space scientist raised from Kolkata, representing India. Now she is in middle school with a lot of achievements and rank in the field of drawing, dance, swimming, basketball and study. And is also a Co-author of "Light & Dark",      "Eso golpo kori", "3rd eye", "the_heritage of Kolkata", "100 splendid words and "TIS". She writes  because she feels that "feelings which we can't express by words can be expressed by writing".

She can be reached through Instagram @the_insomniac_writer

# UNBORN CHILD

Hey!! I came from my father and now I'm in my mother's womb. My parents don't know about me yet. I'm very excited about the day when they'll know about me. Yeahhhh!! My mom-dad came to know about me, they are very happy, I can feel their happiness. My dad is so happy that he took mom for dinner.

I was 2 months then when I got to hear my first heartbeat. Days passed happily. Now I'm of 3 months, I can feel that I'm growing up slowly, I can also feel that my limbs are growing. Everything is going well, my mom-dad even decided my name.

Today I kicked for the first time, my mom screamed with joy. She called daddy and said this and I think daddy was also happy.

Now I'm of 7½ months and I really can't wait to see my mom-dad. Today my mum went to the doctor and she came to know that I am a girl, I thought that she was very happy but I  was wrong. At night when she told my dad this, my dad was shocked, he screamed with anger and then they decided to kill me. After hearing them, I shouted "Mumma!! Mumma!! Don't kill me, I want to see the world...Mumma, please don't kill me" but maybe they couldn't hear me. After a week they went to the doctor, I know the reason but I'm very scared. Once again I shouted "mummmaaaaa don't let me go!! I love you...mum" but all of a sudden everything was blank and I realised, I'm no more.

In the hope of kissing the world,  I kissed heaven.

•STOP KILLING GIRL CHILD

SAVE GIRL CHILD•

# TUITION (A LOVE STORY)

I remember the day. Yes! I do remember each and everything. I was in class 10 at that time and he was in 12. I joined the tuition in class 10, even he joined the tuition when he was in class 10 but that year was his last year. The first day I saw him, I never thought that he would become one of my priorities. The first month of the tuition passed, from the second month we both started talking and by the end of the second month, we became too close. Right from the third month, I started having feelings for him, but as per as I knew, he liked a girl who didn't like him. Even after knowing that, I proposed him. I know its quite irony, like a girl proposing a boy, but that was okay!! He did not say anything except "give me some time". After a week he proposed me with chocolate, everything was going well then. From the fourth month, we couldn't meet during tuitions because of timings and all, even we couldn't talk over calls or texts. But yeah, we used to love each other a lot.

People say long-distance relationship sucks, but have you ever been into a relationship where you can't even talk with the other person?!

# UNDER THE NIGHT SKY

**Imagine**

A night you are sitting with your person, with a bottle of beer. You both indulged in each other, you don't worry about anything and you are totally carefree with that person. That night is only for you both. You both sitting on a bench, under the sky full of stars. While talking, your person suddenly held your hands, a spark of love spread in your body, then you both came closer. Talking about the moon your person looked at you, in turn, you look back, a pure eye contact, then suddenly two lips coming close and boom!! you're wished full filled. Your person took you in your arms and you both spent the night in a different way.

Yes, sometimes love is not just sex, expensive gifts or dates, sometimes its just some care, time and romance.


You felt it right?!

This feeling is amazing